DANGEROUS LOVE

"Todd sure doesn't waste any time, does he?" asked Jessica.

Elizabeth almost dropped the dish she was holding. "I don't know what you're talking about," she declared.

"Come on, Liz, we all saw Mandy get off Todd's bike. You know what I mean."

"I'm not sure I do."

"Well, it's obvious that Todd feels the need to keep the backseat of his motorcycle warm. Didn't you notice the way Mandy was holding on to him as they pulled up? It didn't look so innocent to me."

"There's nothing between Todd and Mandy," Elizabeth insisted.

"Maybe not—now," Jessica conceded. "But I'd keep my eyes open if I were you."

"He was only giving her a ride to school," Elizabeth said, half to herself. "Todd and Mandy are just friends," she added more loudly.

Then why did she feel she had to convince herself?

Bantam Books in the Sweet Valley High Series
Ask your bookseller for the books you have missed

SWEET VALLEY HIGH

DANGEROUS LOVE

Written by
Kate William

Created by
FRANCINE PASCAL

BANTAM BOOKS
TORONTO · NEW YORK · LONDON · SYDNEY · AUCKLAND

RL 6, IL age 12 and up

DANGEROUS LOVE

A Bantam Book / March 1984

2nd printing .... May 1984	5th printing .... May 1985
3rd printing ..... August 1984	6th printing ... September 1985
4th printing ..... October 1984	7th printing ...... March 1986

Sweet Valley High is a trademark of Francine Pascal

Conceived by Francine Pascal

Produced by Cloverdale Press, Inc.

Cover art by James Mathewuse

ISBN 0-553-25105-8

Published simultaneously in the United States and Canada

Bantam Books are published by Bantam Books, Inc. Its trademark,
consisting of the words "Bantam Books" and the portrayal of a rooster,
is Registered in U.S. Patent and Trademark Office and in other
countries. Marca Registrada. Bantam Books, Inc., 666 Fifth Avenue,
New York, New York 10103.

PRINTED IN THE UNITED STATES OF AMERICA

O   16 15 14 13 12 11 10 9 8

DANGEROUS LOVE

One

"I still can't believe you got permission to take the Spider to school today," Jessica Wakefield said, opening the passenger side of the red Fiat convertible. "How'd you do it?"

"Um, I told Mom it was a—a special occasion," her twin sister Elizabeth stammered, sliding in behind the wheel.

Jessica turned the rearview mirror to her side and checked her makeup. She had run late this morning and had dashed out of the Wakefields' split-level house without performing her usual ritual before the bathroom mirror. Not that she really needed it. Tan, blond, with a model-sized waist and a clear, satin-smooth complexion, both she and her identical twin were among the best-looking students at Sweet Valley High.

"What special occasion?" Jessica asked, rummaging in her large leather shoulder bag for her makeup kit.

As Jessica brushed a little more color onto her sun-kissed cheeks, Elizabeth nervously tried to think of something to say. She didn't want to talk about the real reason she was driving to school that day. Jessica would find out soon enough.

"Oh, the reopening of the Dairi Burger," Elizabeth finally blurted out, surprised that she hadn't thought of it before. She returned the mirror to its proper position. "I'm running low this week on information for 'Eyes and Ears,'" she said, referring to the gossip column she wrote for the school newspaper. "I figure everyone's going to be there, so there should be plenty to write about."

Jessica eyed her sister with skepticism. There was something in Elizabeth's voice that made Jessica suspect that her twin was being less than honest with her. "I'd hardly call the reopening of that grease pit the event of the century. Besides, I'd think you'd have all the info you could use from the surfing championship that Bill Chase won." As she talked, Jessica held a pocket mirror in one hand and combed out her shoulder-length hair with the other.

"That was last week, remember?"

Jessica groaned as she put away her comb and reached for her lipstick. "Please don't remind me," she said, the memory of the case of poison oak that had kept her home still fresh in her mind. Where did Elizabeth find the time to get ready? she wondered. Her hair tied back with a blue ribbon, dressed in jeans, blue oxford shirt, and dark blue blazer, Elizabeth looked as fresh and attractive as could be. But then, Jessica reflected, Elizabeth didn't bother with much makeup, using only a tiny hint of blush and mascara.

Jessica sighed. She rolled down her window to catch some of the early-morning breeze. Although it was only eight o'clock, the air was already warming under the bright sun. It was going to be another gorgeous day in Sweet Valley. "Hey, Liz," Jessica said excitedly, "let's take down the top."

"No!" Elizabeth answered a bit too sharply.

"Why not?"

"It's just not a good idea," Elizabeth said with uncharacteristic edginess.

"Sounds like I touched a raw nerve," Jessica noted. "What's with you this morning? Here it is a beautiful day, and we've got the car and—"

3

Jessica stopped herself. "Hey, why *do* we have the car?"

"I told you—to go to the Dairi Burger."

"No, no, I mean what happened to Todd?" she asked. "How come you're not going to the Dairi Burger with him?"

"How do you know I'm not?" Elizabeth asked.

Jessica pressed on. "He's got his own set of wheels, doesn't he? Or are you playing chauffeur for the day?"

"No, it's nothing like that."

"Then what is it, Liz?" Jessica insisted. "Will you please tell me what's going on?"

Elizabeth waited until she reached the stop sign at the corner before answering. "Todd's not driving his car anymore."

"He what—?" Jessica said before remembering. "You mean he finally bought that motorcycle he's been talking about?"

Elizabeth nodded. "He was supposed to get it Friday, but there was some delay, so he picked it up last night. He's driving it to school today."

"I should have known," Jessica said, not bothering to hide her dislike for Elizabeth's boyfriend. The two had been at odds with each other ever since Todd had rejected Jessica for her sister. "I really don't believe that guy," she continued. "Here he is, claiming to love you so much, yet he goes off and gets that awful machine when he knows that you can't—"

Elizabeth quickly cut her sister off. "He doesn't know," she said quietly.

"What do you mean?"

"I mean, I didn't tell him yet," Elizabeth admitted. "He thinks I'm as excited about the bike as he is."

"How could you?" Jessica was shocked at her sister's deception. Not that fibbing was a foreign concept to her—Jessica had often stretched the truth when it served her purposes—but that Elizabeth had felt the need to be less than forthright truly puzzled her. Elizabeth was the most honest and straightforward person she knew. Jessica would have expected her to be especially up-front on this issue, a subject that had been discussed at length in the Wakefield household and one on which Jessica herself had very strong opinions. Motorcycles were nothing but death machines as far as Jessica was concerned, and she would have been perfectly happy if every single one were banned from the universe. She was sure Elizabeth felt the same way—at least she had been until right then. Was love blinding her sister's good sense?

"I mean, after Rexy, how can you even consider getting near one of those things?" Jessica asked.

"I'm not, Jess. I have no intention of ever riding on that motorcycle. And I hate the thought of Todd on it, too. But how could I tell him that? He's been fantasizing about this bike for years. I couldn't bear the thought of shattering his dream."

"But you wouldn't mind if he shattered his body? Come on, Lizzie, be sensible!"

Ordinarily Elizabeth would have chuckled at Jessica's advice. After all, she'd told Jessica to be sensible more times than she cared to count. But this time she knew Jessica had a point.

Their cousin Rexy Wakefield had been a bright, handsome boy who had everything in the world going for him. Then, three years ago, a few days after his sixteenth birthday, he bought himself a motorcycle, despite his parents' objections. The following day he was killed in a head-on collision with a station wagon. His death was a blow to all of them, particularly to Jessica, who'd adored Rexy almost as much as she did Steven, her older brother. Afterward, their parents made them swear they'd never ride on a motorcycle. It was a rule they all obeyed, one of the few that Jessica obeyed willingly.

When Todd first mentioned getting a motorcycle, Elizabeth had dismissed it as just talk. But as his bank account grew and his talk continued, Elizabeth had come to understand how serious he was. She knew it was time to tell Todd about Rexy and her inability to share his dream. But she couldn't. He'd taken her silence as merely fear of the unknown and had assured her that the first time she got on the bike with him, all her fears would disappear.

If Elizabeth had been a different kind of person, not only would she have spoken up sooner, she would have begged Todd not to buy the motorcycle in the first place. But she felt strongly that she didn't have the right to impose her own restrictions on Todd—though if she had done so, she would certainly be sleeping better at night. Even at this very moment she was filled with worry over whether he'd get to school safely.

"Look, Jess," Elizabeth told her twin after much thought, "Todd's bike is just something I'm going to have to learn to accept."

"And ride with him?" Jessica asked, her blue-green eyes wide in amazement.

"Of course not!" Elizabeth exclaimed. "One has nothing to do with the other."

"Oh, no?" Jessica shot back. "Don't be a fool, Liz. Look at the reality. That bike has a backseat. What are you going to tell him when he asks you to ride with him?"

"He already did. He wanted to pick me up this morning."

"And how did you get out of that?"

"I told him I felt a cold coming on, and it wouldn't be a good idea to expose myself to the wind."

"So that's why you didn't want to put the top

down. Great." Jessica shook her thick blond mane. "That's fine for today, Liz, but what are you going to tell him tomorrow—or the next day?"

Elizabeth hit the steering wheel in frustration. "Look, I know I've got to tell him the truth. I'm just afraid of what he might say."

Seeing her sister's distress, Jessica decided to back down. She put her hand on Elizabeth's shoulder and said, "Liz, Todd may not be my most favorite person in the world, but I know he cares for you enough not to let the bike interfere with your relationship."

"I'm not so sure, Jess. . . ."

"You can't put it off, Liz," Jessica warned, her voice growing harder. "The more excuses you make to Todd, the more he's going to think something's wrong. He might as well know the truth now, before he starts to think it's *him* you're turned off to."

Her sister hadn't said anything that Elizabeth hadn't thought about before, but hearing it so plainly made her realize what she had to do. She was just about to say so when Jessica added, "Of course, I can't see why you'd want to continue a relationship with a motorcycle maniac—especially when there are so many great guys around who drive cars."

"Like Danny and his Trans-Am?" Elizabeth

asked. Danny Stauffer was a boy that Jessica had just started to go out with.

"Exactly. You said yourself how handsome and terrific he is. Maybe this is just the excuse you need to check out your options."

Elizabeth smiled ruefully. She knew Jessica had a hard time understanding just how much she loved Todd. Her sister hadn't yet experienced such a deep and caring relationship with any of her many boyfriends. But in her own way Jessica had gotten her to see how important it was to tell Todd the truth. Jessica was right, Elizabeth concluded. If Todd loved her, he would understand.

Todd hadn't yet arrived when Elizabeth pulled into the Sweet Valley High parking lot. But as soon as she stepped out of the car, she spotted Enid Rollins, her best friend, getting off the school bus. Enid held a thick stack of books close to her side and walked along slowly, her round face slightly lowered, as scores of carefree kids flew right by her.

Elizabeth had often wished that others could see what a bright and witty person Enid was, but it was a side that the normally reserved brunette revealed to only a handful of people. Perhaps it was because she was the youngest junior in the class. She had skipped a grade when she was in elementary school and, as a result, had been subjected to much teasing by her older classmates. Elizabeth was one of the few people she confided in, as was Enid's boyfriend, George Warren, a freshman at Sweet Valley College.

Elizabeth waved to get her attention. "Enid!"

Jessica looked at her sister with undisguised pity. Elizabeth was the type of person who never gave up on a lost cause, and Jessica felt that Enid was a prime example. For the life of her she couldn't figure out what the two of them had in common.

Enid brightened a bit when she saw Elizabeth. "Hi, Liz," she said, pointedly ignoring Jessica. "I've got to talk to you."

The two friends had spent the better part of the previous day's gym class going over the dilemma with Todd, and Elizabeth hoped Enid wouldn't bring it up again this morning. She was all talked out.

She needn't have worried. "You won't believe the number my mom pulled on me this morning," Enid said dejectedly. "I was on my way out of the house when she told me I've got to rush home right after school and address invitations to my party!"

"What for?" Jessica asked incredulously. "You've already invited half the school!"

"I know," Enid said, "but Mom's insistent. She said a special occasion like my sixteenth birthday deserves special treatment. So she went out and got these incredibly fancy engraved invitations. Can you believe it?"

"For your silly little party?" Jessica wondered.

Enid's face turned beet red. She never quite knew how to answer one of Jessica's put-downs.

This time Elizabeth came to her rescue. "If it's so silly, Jess, how come you're going?"

"Oh, never mind," Jessica said, looking ahead toward the white columns that flanked the entrance to the massive brick building. "I think I see Cara up there. I've got to talk to her. See you later, Liz."

As Jessica dashed off to her own best friend, Enid stuck her tongue out at her, making sure Elizabeth didn't notice.

"Well, I think the invitations are a nice idea," Elizabeth said. "They show how much your mother cares for you."

"I'd rather be spending my time at the Dairi Burger," Enid grumbled.

Elizabeth's response was drowned out by the roar of a motorcycle engine. Todd's motorcycle. Her stomach churned as a mixture of emotions rushed through her. She was glad he'd made it to school safely, but his arrival also meant that she'd come to the moment of truth. She had to tell him she couldn't ride with him.

It was going to be difficult. If possible, Todd was even more attractive than ever that morning, cutting a sexy, self-assured pose astride his shiny black bike. He was wearing a soft leather jacket, which hugged his long, trim body, and a black full-faced helmet, which he now took off to reveal his tousled head of dark brown hair and the biggest smile Elizabeth had seen on his face for ages.

"Well, how do you like it?" he asked, directing his gaze at his girlfriend. "A Yamaha 750 Virago. It's a beauty, isn't it?"

Before Elizabeth could answer, they were joined by Guy Chesney and Max Dellon, members of Sweet Valley High's most popular band, The Droids.

"It sure is," Max said, caressing one of the handlebars. "Pretty powerful, huh?"

Todd proudly patted the teardrop-shaped gas tank. "It's as much as I'll ever need," he answered.

"Very impressive, Wilkins," said Guy. "I suppose you'll be going everywhere on that from now on."

"As long as it doesn't rain, this is where you'll find me."

"Boy, are you going to have fun, Liz," said Guy, turning to face her.

Elizabeth nodded absently, her gaze now focused on something else, a hot-pink helmet attached to the side of the bike. *Her* helmet, she presumed, another wave of dread washing over her. Telling Todd the truth was going to be very hard.

"Well, Liz," Todd repeated, "what do you think of it? Want to take a little spin before the bell rings?"

"I can't, Todd," she answered, hastily checking her watch. "I just remembered, I'm supposed to meet Mr. Collins in the *Oracle* office before first period. Got to run. See you." She gave him a quick kiss on the cheek. Then she turned to her best friend. "I'll talk to you later, Enid."

Two

Elizabeth was the first person out of her math class after the bell rang. She had to find Todd and explain why she had run from him earlier in the morning. She had to tell him before it was too late. Jessica was right. Putting it off might be fatal to their relationship.

Fatal. Elizabeth cringed at the word. Ever since Rexy's death, the words *fatal* and *motorcycle* were synonymous to her. Rationally, she knew that was silly—she saw lots of cyclists riding safely down the streets of Sweet Valley every day. Yet that emotional reaction was hard to shake. She couldn't quite get it out of her mind that all people who rode motorcycles were flirting with death. But she knew she had to stop feeling that way. For Todd's sake.

Where was Todd? She didn't find him on the cafeteria line, nor was he joking around with his basketball buddies on the outdoor patio. Despairingly, Elizabeth approached the table occupied by several of Jessica's friends.

"Liz, have you heard anything about the tryouts for the school play?" Lila Fowler asked before she had a chance to say anything.

"I think that's still a few weeks away, Lila. Listen, you haven't seen Todd around, have you?"

"Have you tried the lost and found?" Lila purred.

"Lay off her, Lila," said Cara Walker. "I think she's serious. Is anything wrong, Liz?"

"I just have to speak to him. Do you have any idea where he might be?"

"Hey, Liz," said Ken Matthews, overhearing the conversation as he passed by the table with his lunch tray. "If you're looking for Todd, you'll find him in the parking lot with his new toy."

"Thanks, Ken," Elizabeth said, giving her favorite football player a squeeze on the arm. "You're an angel."

A few minutes later Elizabeth approached Todd, who was busily polishing the Yamaha's gleaming chrome exhaust pipes. "Oh, hi, Liz," he said, looking up at the sound of her footsteps. "I can't believe how much dirt I picked up just riding to school. I'm going to have to spend all my spare time keeping this baby clean." He dropped his rag and gave Elizabeth a hug. "How's my favorite motorcycle mama?"

That was the last thing she needed to hear. Feeling her determination slip a little, she released herself from his strong grasp, then looked him in the eye. "Look, Todd, I'm sorry I ran out on you this morning. I—"

"Hey, what's the big deal?" Todd interrupted good-naturedly. "You had work to do. I can understand that."

"Thanks," Elizabeth said. "I—"

Todd cut her off again. "I'm just sorry I didn't get a chance to give you this." He bent down to unlatch the pink helmet from its perch on the side of the bike. "I thought you'd look terrific in hot pink. The guy in the shop looked at me kind of funny when I told him I wanted pink, but when I said it was for my girlfriend, he said I had excellent taste. Here, try it on." Rising, he held out the helmet to Elizabeth, but she wouldn't take it.

"I—can't," she said haltingly.

Todd refused to be bothered by her hesitation. "Look, if you're worried about making your cold worse, you don't have to ride with me now. I just want to see how the helmet looks."

"No, Todd, I don't want to."

"Hey, don't tell me you're afraid of messing up your hair. Now, if it was Jessica, I could understand it, but you. . . . Hey, what's the matter, Liz?" Todd asked, noticing the tears welling in her eyes.

"I don't have a cold, Todd," Elizabeth admitted. "I made that up."

"Why?" Todd asked, a puzzled expression on his face.

"It was easier to tell you that than to tell you I can't ride with you. And not just today, Todd. I mean ever."

"You can't?" Todd exclaimed, nearly dropping the helmet. "Why not?"

Elizabeth took a deep breath and said, "A few years ago a cousin of mine, Rexy, died in a motorcycle accident. Since then my parents have forbidden us from ever riding on one."

"How come you've waited till now to tell me this?" Todd said brusquely, setting the helmet on the motorcycle's black leather seat. "You knew for months I was getting a bike."

"I was afraid of how you'd react."

Todd ran his fingers through his thick brown hair. "You mean that you thought I'd choose the bike over you or something?" After Elizabeth nodded yes, Todd shook his head and gave her the smile that Elizabeth always found so appealing. "Come here, you little fool," he

17

said, drawing her close. "Do you really think you mean so little to me that I'd drop you for refusing to get on this machine?"

When he put it that way, Elizabeth suddenly felt silly for having been so worried. "Well . . ." she began.

"Say no more," he said, putting a finger over her lips. Then he replaced that finger with his own lips and kissed her with unmistakable intensity. "Now do you have any doubts about what you are to me?"

"Oh, Todd," Elizabeth said with great relief, "you do understand, don't you!"

"About how you feel about me, yes. About how you feel about riding my motorcycle, yes again. If I had a tragedy like that in my family, I'd probably feel the same way you do. I guess you probably don't like my having this bike at all."

"I'm worried about you," Elizabeth said honestly, "but I know how much it means to you. I'd never want you not to ride just because of me."

Todd let out a sigh of relief. "I'm glad you feel that way," he said, giving her a quick kiss on the nose, "because I have no intention of giving it up. Besides, one thing that people unfamiliar with motorcycles don't realize is that the overwhelming majority of accidents happen to people who don't know how to ride or are improperly protected. I'm a good driver, Liz. And I'm always careful. What happened to your cousin was terrible, and I'm sorry for your family, but I'm even sorrier for you because you'll never know the other side, the joy of being on one of these two-wheelers."

"You think I'm missing out on something really special, huh?"

"I know you are. When the weather's warm and sunny like it is today, believe me, there's no better way to travel. I could take you into the hills, and you'd feel the wind wrapping around you. You'd be able to look around and see the trees, the birds, even the road in a way you never have before. You'd actually be part of the scenery, not just watching it. It's the kind of experience you never get when you're cooped up in a car." Todd's brown eyes were sparkling with excitement.

Elizabeth looked back at the bike. She wished she could share Todd's joy, but she couldn't imagine how he could be relaxed and comfortable and enjoy the view when his life depended on being able to balance five hundred pounds between his legs at fifty-five miles per hour. But there was more to it than that. His choice of color disturbed her as well. Black. The color of death. For a brief second a picture of Rexy flashed across her mind.

Quickly she shook off the thought. *There's no*

connection, she repeated to herself. *What happened to Rexy doesn't have to happen to Todd.*

Todd continued to watch her as she stared at his bike. "It still scares you, doesn't it?" It was more of a statement than a question.

"Yes," Elizabeth acknowledged.

"You may not believe this," said Todd, putting his hand on her shoulder, "but I understand. I was a little nervous myself the first time I got on one of these things. But it's not like you think."

"Don't you ever worry about falling off?"

"No, the bike practically stands up by itself. The only way anything can happen to me is if I'm careless. And I don't plan to be."

"Nobody ever plans an accident," she reminded him.

"The Elizabeth Wakefield I know is cautious, practical, and methodical," Todd said, a trace of frustration creeping into his voice, "but she's not a worrier. Why are you so sure that only the worst can happen? Your cousin's death was a tragedy, but what happened to him doesn't happen to everyone who rides."

"I know," Elizabeth said. "But it's going to take some getting used to."

Todd waited awhile before continuing. "If your parents were to change their minds and lift their restrictions, do you think you'd ever consider riding with me?"

Elizabeth didn't look at him as she spoke.

20

"They'll never change their minds. They loved Rexy, and they love us too much to let us risk our lives."

"It doesn't have to be that way, Liz. I sure don't think I'm putting my life on the line every time I rev that engine. Look, do you mind if I speak to them? Maybe if they hear how safe it can be, they'll reconsider."

When Elizabeth looked into Todd's pleading eyes, she knew she couldn't stand to disappoint him one more time. Even though she felt it would be pointless, she nodded. "OK, you can ask them. There's certainly no harm in that."

"Tonight?"

"So soon?" The words escaped her lips before she realized how abrupt they sounded. "OK. Tonight's fine," she relented. "How's seven-thirty?"

She wasn't prepared for the big smile that crossed his face. "Thanks, Liz," he said, squeezing her tightly again. "You won't regret it, believe me."

"I'm not so sure that thanks are warranted," she said, adding, "Look, if we're going to get some lunch, we'd better hurry. Only fifteen minutes left."

"Is that all?" Todd glanced at his watch to check the time. "Gosh, I've got to run."

"We can walk and still have time to eat."

Todd looked a little flustered as he said, "I'm

sorry, Liz. I can't eat with you today. I promised Mandy and Winston I'd meet with them."

"What for?"

"Mr. Marks grouped us together for a project in current events. An overview of the Save the Whales movement—and he gave us only a few days to do it in."

"Sounds like you're going to be a very busy guy."

"But never too busy for you, Liz. See you at the Dairi Burger later?"

As she watched him run across the parking lot, Elizabeth smiled with relief. Todd had been so understanding. She had a feeling that everything was going to work out fine.

Three

The Dairi Burger lot was already more than half filled by the time Elizabeth pulled in with the Fiat. Finding an empty space near the drive-through area, she parked and took her first look at the refurbished restaurant.

The Doherty brothers had outdone themselves, she thought, impressed by the way the restaurant owners had turned the popular though somewhat shabby-looking hangout into a respectable restaurant. The most visible improvement was the replacement of the dingy, white-tiled exterior with natural wood planking. The neon sign atop the roof, which used to read

D RI URGE, was gone, too, and in its place was a brown plastic sign with the words spelled out in yellow script letters.

The inside had a completely new style as well, redone in the wood-and-plants look so popular with many of the area's eateries. Elizabeth didn't think the plants had a chance of lasting more than a week, but she felt that the new wooden booths and tables were a welcome replacement for the old cracked red vinyl and Formica, covered with the graffiti of close to a generation of Sweet Valley students. Behind the counter the Dohertys had put up a new order board that stretched the entire length of the wall. To the right of the counter was the door to the newly created game room, which now contained the half dozen or so video games that had previously been scattered haphazardly around the room.

In celebration of the opening, the entire interior was decorated with multicolored streamers and helium-filled balloons sporting the Dairi Burger logo. Beside the entrance were two boxes containing T-shirts and bumper stickers reading "I love Dairi Burger," with the love signified by a big red heart. Elizabeth picked up one of each, then squeezed her way through the crowd to one of the few remaining empty tables. She reserved the spot, leaving her blue cotton blazer behind before taking her place on line at the order counter.

As she waited, she let her gaze wander around the room. The scene here had enough action to fill a semester's worth of "Eyes and Ears" columns, she thought. Over at a table near the center of the room, where he knew he'd be seen, Sweet Valley's popular Bruce Patman was entertaining a beautiful, long-haired brunette Elizabeth didn't know. Her hunch was that she was probably someone from a neighboring high school, though knowing Bruce as she did, the girl could just as likely have been a student at the university. Cara Walker, Jessica's best friend, was sitting at a small booth near the counter sharing an order of the Dairi Burger's newest dish, the hot clam special, with John Pfeifer, one of Elizabeth's co-workers on *The Oracle*. She made a mental note to ask Jessica later if they were anything more than just friends. In the adjoining booth, Bill Chase was surrounded by a horde of girls, clearly enjoying the newfound status he'd garnered by winning the big surfing championship.

Robin Wilson and her boyfriend Allen Walters were there, too. They waved to Elizabeth as she carried her food back to her table. "Come join us," Robin called.

"Thanks, but I'm waiting for Todd," Elizabeth told her.

"Didn't I see Todd on his new motorcycle today?" Robin asked. "How come you're not riding with him?"

"Oh—um—I have the Fiat today," Elizabeth said, avoiding the real reason.

In deference to the opening, Elizabeth decided to forgo her favorite chili dog and try the new special. It looked good, she thought as she put the first forkful into her mouth, but the concoction of clams and a mysterious batter was as heavy as a lead bullet. The Dohertys needed to work on it more, she concluded, jotting down her impressions of the dish as she washed away its slightly bitter taste with her root beer.

Putting down her cup, she looked toward the parking lot. Todd should have arrived by now. What was keeping him? she wondered. But just as she began to imagine him lying in a heap on the road with his bike beside him, she stopped herself short. *You've got to trust him*, she told herself. Todd was a good driver and very responsible. Nothing was going to happen to him. *Besides*, she added silently, *if I don't start trusting him, I'm going to go crazy with worry*.

Before she had a chance to dwell any further on Todd's whereabouts, she saw Danny Stauffer's red Trans-Am roar into the newly blacktopped parking lot, with Jessica sitting in the bucket seat beside him.

Danny had been driving fast, and he slammed

on his brakes a little too late. The brakes locked just before the car bumped into the rear fender of a big purple van. It didn't look as if any damage had been done, but the impact shook the van a little and got its owner, Jerry "Crunch" McAllister, very upset. Within seconds, he was out of the van and heading toward Danny's car.

"Uh-oh, Danny's in for it now," Elizabeth muttered as she rose from her seat and made her way toward the parking lot.

They didn't call Jerry McAllister "Crunch" for nothing. As starting tackle on the Sweet Valley High football team, Crunch McAllister had rolled over the opposition handily until his playing career was cut short by a knee injury. Unable to play anymore and never much of a student, Crunch had dropped out of school several months earlier. He worked every now and then on construction jobs but spent most of his time at places like the Dairi Burger or, more often, at bars like the Shady Lady across the street. Despite his age, he never had trouble getting beers. And when Crunch had too many beers inside him, anything could happen.

Elizabeth didn't know if Crunch had been drinking or not, but her concern was for Danny and Jessica, who were still inside the car.

Danny rolled down his window when he saw Crunch's menacing face staring at him. "Hey."

Danny grinned weakly. "No damage, done, right?"

"Get out," Crunch grunted.

A small crowd had already gathered to watch the drama unfold. "Ten to one says Crunch decks him," Bruce Patman said, clearly relishing the prospect of a brawl.

Why don't you stop him? Elizabeth wanted to snap back. But she knew Bruce would never willingly expose himself to bodily harm—especially in defense of someone else.

Fear showing through his thin facade of bravado, Danny got out of his car and faced the much taller, much more muscular boy. Seeing her chance to escape, Jessica got out the other door and quickly ran to her sister's side. "I think he's going to kill Danny," she predicted.

Crunch grabbed Danny by the front of his jacket and led him to the van's rear fender. "Look what you did!" he roared.

Danny relaxed a bit when he saw how little damage there actually was. "It's just a tiny dent. You can hardly see it," he said, pulling away from Crunch.

"Maybe you need your eyes checked, buddy. *I* see it real good," Crunch shot back. "Look!" He grabbed Danny's jacket again and dragged him around the rest of the van. "Not a dent, not a mark, not even a scratch anywhere. Perfection—until you came along."

As frightened as Danny was, he was grateful there wasn't a trace of alcohol on Crunch's breath. If Crunch got this steamed up sober, Danny couldn't imagine how he would have reacted with a few beers under his belt. It was bad enough when Crunch led him back to his Trans-Am and threw him against the side of its front fender.

"I don't take kindly to wimps messing with my wheels," Crunch warned.

Crunch hadn't thrown him too hard, but Danny still closed his eyes, afraid of what was going to happen next. Although he was in fairly good shape, he knew he was no match for the powerful, muscular Crunch, who had grabbed the back of his jacket and was about to throw him against the car again. He opened his eyes to look toward Jessica. Any chance he might have had with her was gone, he realized. Jessica went for winners. And there was no way he was going to win this bout. He only hoped that Crunch would end it quickly.

Suddenly a loud noise attracted Crunch's attention, and he let go of Danny's jacket and walked over to the source of the sound: a shiny black motorcycle that had pulled up alongside the Dairi Burger entrance.

It was Todd. And he wasn't alone.

"Some wheels," Crunch said, impressed. "Virago, right?"

"You bet." Todd took off his helmet and rested it on the gas tank.

"Man, I've been drooling for a bike like this."

"Want to ride it?" Todd offered.

Crunch couldn't believe his good fortune. "Could I?" he aked, suddenly sounding like a little boy who'd been handed the key to a candy store.

Todd handed Crunch his helmet as he jumped off the bike. But Elizabeth's attention was directed toward the person who got off the bike with him. It was Mandy Farmer, the girl who was saving the whales with Todd. As the tall, shapely girl took off the helmet she was wearing and let her long, black hair wave in the breeze, Elizabeth began to shake.

Mandy had been wearing a hot pink helmet. Elizabeth's helmet.

Elizabeth tried hard to suppress the feelings of jealousy that now were welling up inside her. She knew she had no reason to feel this way, but the sight of the attractive girl holding Todd's waist unnerved her. She tried to erase the image from her mind. *It's silly to let it bother me*, she told herself. *Mandy's my friend.*

Quickly she joined the rest of the crowd now surrounding Todd.

"You saved my life," she heard Danny say gratefully as he shook Todd's hand.

Unaware of the scene that preceded him, Todd was perplexed. "All I did was offer Crunch a ride. What's the big deal?"

"I'll tell you." Elizabeth stepped forward, forcing herself to smile. "You rode in here like a knight in shining armor, that's what," she said, giving him a kiss. Despite her conflicting emotions, she *was* proud of him.

Crunch returned with the bike a few minutes later and dismounted with surprising agility. "You're a lucky guy," he told Todd. "If you ever want to sell this baby, just let me know."

"Don't hold your breath, Crunch," Todd answered, bending over to secure his helmet to the bike. "I plan to hold on to this bike until it dies of old age. But if you ever want to take it for another spin, just let me know."

"Thanks, Todd. See ya around." With a wave of his hand, Crunch turned and headed toward his van. Then, remembering he had some unfinished business to attend to, he turned around and glared at Danny. Apparently satisfied by the look of terror that once again crossed Danny's face, Crunch merely smirked and called out, "Next time watch where you're going, or you'll *really* have a reason to be scared."

And with that he was off.

Mandy was handing Todd her helmet as John Doherty, one of the Dairi Burger's owners, came up to him. "I could have ended up with a lawsuit on my hands if it hadn't been for you. Come on in," he said, smiling. "To show my appreciation I'm going to give you and your girlfriend a free hot clam special!"

Elizabeth groaned inwardly at the thought of having to down another one of those torpedoes, but it quickly became clear that the offer wasn't meant for her. John Doherty had grabbed both Todd and Mandy by the arm and was leading them to the restaurant.

Before they got to the door, though, Todd stopped him. "Thanks for the offer, but that's my girl," he said, pointing to Elizabeth.

"Very well, then," John said, grinning. "Free specials for you and your *two* lovely ladies."

Todd rolled his eyes toward Elizabeth as they all entered the Dairi Burger.

That night the twins were in the kitchen cleaning up after dinner. Elizabeth was rinsing the dishes while Jessica was loading the dishwasher. Jessica hadn't had a chance to be alone with her sister since she got home, and she was dying for the lowdown on what had gone on that afternoon.

But Elizabeth didn't seem interested in volunteering the details of her conversation with Todd. Jessica could see she'd have to be the one to speak up first.

"Todd sure doesn't waste any time, does he?" she said. Her contempt for Todd was thick enough to cut with a knife.

Elizabeth almost dropped the dish in her hand. "I don't know what you're talking about," she declared, staring down at the dirty dinner plate as if it were the most important thing on earth.

"Come on, Liz, we all saw Mandy get off that bike with Todd. You know what I mean."

"I'm not sure I do."

"Well, it's obvious that Todd feels the need to keep the backseat of his bike warm."

Elizabeth carefully rinsed the plate before handing it to her sister. "Oh, Jess, you're just jumping to conclusions. Give me a break, OK?"

But Jessica was undeterred. She knew Elizabeth would let the problem fester inside her unless Jessica forced her to talk about it. The last thing in the world Jessica wanted was to see her twin get hurt, and as long as Todd had that motorcycle, she saw nothing but trouble ahead. "Listen, Elizabeth," Jessica continued, "didn't you notice the way Mandy was holding on to Todd as they pulled up? It didn't look so innocent to me."

"How else was she supposed to stay on the bike?" Elizabeth snapped back as she handed Jessica another plate. But even though Todd had explained it to her, she was still upset. And she didn't like feeling that way at all. "It was no big deal," she added, echoing Todd's earlier words. "She and Todd are working on a class project together. So he gave her a lift. He was just being friendly."

"*You* may see it that way, but *I* don't. A guy who's 'just being friendly,' wouldn't let a girl drape herself all over him like that, and you know it. In case you haven't noticed, those bikes have arm rails on them."

"I didn't know you knew so much about motorcycles."

Jessica took the saucepan from her sister and examined the nearly full dishwasher. "Where am I going to fit this?" she mumbled to herself, finally rearranging several dishes to make the pot fit. Looking back at Elizabeth, she continued, "Let's just say that I know enough about them to know I wouldn't tolerate *my* boyfriend riding one."

"I don't like it any better than you do, but I respect Todd's wishes enough not to force any demands on him. I'm willing to accept his bike riding, just as he's willing to accept my reasons for not riding with him."

"Well, at least I'd ask him not to give lifts to strange girls."

"Mandy's hardly a strange girl. She's your sorority sister."

"Even sorority sisters aren't above stealing someone else's boyfriend."

"There's nothing between Todd and Mandy," Elizabeth insisted.

"Maybe not—now," Jessica conceded, "but I'd keep my eyes open if I were you."

"You're making too much out of this," Elizabeth said. "Anyway, Todd's coming over tonight to talk to Mom and Dad. He wants to try to convince them to change their rule."

Jessica closed the dishwasher door with a thud. "You don't mean to tell me you're actually thinking about getting on that motorcycle!"

"Well, no . . ." Elizabeth wavered. "But Todd insists it's safe. And lots of people ride around without getting hurt."

"And a lot of others get killed—like Rexy!" Jessica shouted angrily.

"Jess, please calm down—"

"I'm not sticking around to listen to you talk about that death machine. If anyone wants me, I'll be at Cara's!" Jessica turned on her heel and stormed out of the room.

Elizabeth understood Jessica's anger. But Todd was right, too. The bike could be looked at as simply a means of transportation, no more dangerous than a car, in the right hands. Accidents happened to people who drove cars, too, and she didn't go around worrying every time she saw a car go by.

How could two of the people she loved the most both be right, she wondered, and both be on opposite sides?

And where did that leave her?

Four

Several hours later Jessica opened the front door of the Wakefield house, stole inside, and listened silently to the conversation going on in the living room.

"We appreciate your coming over tonight," her father was saying. "Most boys in your situation wouldn't have bothered, I suspect."

"But that doesn't change your mind, does it, sir?"

"No, Todd, I'm afraid it doesn't. I'm sure you're a capable driver, and you've impressed us with your concern for safety. But I still can't allow my daughter to ride with you."

"I hope you understand, Todd," added Alice Wakefield.

"Of course. I agree with you that Liz's safety is the most important thing. I'd hoped to convince you that she'd be safe with me, but I can understand your fears. You have my word that you'll never see your daughter on my bike."

"Thank you, Todd," Ned Wakefield said. "That's one promise I'm going to hold you to."

Todd rose from his chair. "It's getting late, and I still have some homework to do. Good night, Mr. and Mrs. Wakefield. Liz, want to walk me to the door?"

Elizabeth rose from the sofa, where she had listened silently while Todd and her parents had debated her fate. In a funny way she was relieved that the decision wasn't hers to make. She joined Todd for the short walk to the front hallway. Jessica, meanwhile, had tiptoed, unseen, up to her room.

"I had to try," Todd said, cupping her hands in his. "But it won't make any difference, I promise."

She was relieved to hear him say that. "It doesn't matter how we get to and from places as long as we're together the rest of the time, right?"

"Right," Todd agreed. Pulling her close, he

looked tenderly into her aquamarine eyes. Then, with a hint of a smile he asked, "Say, do you think your parents would mind if I kissed you in their hallway—or should I ask their permission first?"

Elizabeth picked up his cue. "There are some things a girl can do without parental approval," she said, trying to imitate Jessica's attitude of carefree abandon. "And this is one of them." Wrapping her arms around Todd's well-muscled torso, she proceeded to demonstrate that riding a motorcycle wasn't the only kind of fun available to him.

"Hmm, maybe I'll stay a little while longer," Todd said.

"No, we both have work to do," Elizabeth reasoned. "I'll see you tomorrow. And, Todd?" She looked lovingly into his eyes. "Could you do me a favor?"

"Anything."

"Would you call me as soon as you get home?"

Todd knew immediately that the request stemmed from the worry Elizabeth still couldn't quite shake. "Sure," he said, tousling her hair. "And I'll drive extra slowly, too."

Elizabeth lingered at the door for a few minutes after Todd left before heading upstairs to her room. It was only now that Todd was gone that she realized just how relieved she was that her parents had stuck by their rule. That big black-and-chrome machine truly scared her. Sighing, she sorted through the books on her desk for her French notebook. There was nothing better than work to blot out the day's events. But before she had a chance to start her homework, Jessica barged in.

"Liz, I was just wondering about something," she announced.

"I'm not riding with Todd," Elizabeth answered, quickly looking down at her notebook. The last thing she wanted to do was hash out the subject of Todd and his bike for the umpteenth time that day.

But Jessica's earlier eavesdropping had convinced her that the motorcycle was now a dead issue. "That's not what I came to talk about," she declared impatiently.

Surprised, Elizabeth turned around in her chair and eyed her sister. "Then what is?" she asked.

"Enid's cousin Brian," Jessica announced with a flourish, plopping down in the middle of Elizabeth's neatly made bed.

Elizabeth remained frozen in her seat. "What about him?"

"Is he going to be in town for Enid's party?"

Elizabeth thought for a moment. "Now that you mention it, I think Enid said he'd be there. She's his favorite cousin, you know."

"I bet Enid's thrilled he's coming," Jessica remarked, appearing to take a sudden interest in Elizabeth's friend. "He's still at UCLA, isn't he?"

"Yes, a sophomore."

"How fortunate." Jessica let the words slip out.

"For whom?" Elizabeth's eyebrows shot up.

"For me—that is, if you'll help me." Jessica turned her doe-eyed, innocent face toward her sister. "Will you ask Enid to fix me up with him for the party?"

Elizabeth sighed. "I was afraid of that."

"Afraid of what?" The innocence disappeared, and Jessica's face took on a hard, haughty look of mortally wounded pride. "Afraid of ruining Brian's time by setting him up with some high school reject?"

"That's not what I meant, and you know it," Elizabeth said, wishing she could pretend this day had never started. She'd known that sooner or later the time was going to come when she'd be squeezed between her sister and her best friend, but Jessica had really picked an awful time to spring this on her. With the motorcycle business preying on her mind, she wasn't sure if she could think clearly enough to step across this potential mine field. If she slipped, she risked offending one of them. Or maybe both. "I was afraid of your asking me to have Enid do you a favor. After what you did to her, Jess, it's really not fair. . . ."

"I get it." Jessica sniffled and turned that innocent look back on. "So I told an old boyfriend of hers about her less than perfect past. I admit it. But that was a long time ago. Is that one mistake supposed to follow me around and torture me for the rest of my life? I could understand how Enid might see it that way, but I hardly expected you to agree."

"I don't." Elizabeth sighed wearily. Once again she felt herself getting sucked into another sticky situation courtesy of Jessica.

"Besides," Jessica continued, "if Ronnie hadn't dumped her because of what I told him, she wouldn't have gotten back together with George. He's the one she really wanted in the first place, right?"

"Right." Elizabeth had to agree.

"So actually I ended up doing Enid a favor. She owes me one," Jessica concluded.

Elizabeth shook her head at her twin's twisted logic. "You've missed the point, Jessica. It's easy for you to talk now that everything's worked out fine for Enid. But I don't recall you having such sympathy for her at the time."

"Oh, am I going to get a lecture from you now, too?" Jessica threw her arms in the air. "What did I do to deserve this?"

"Calm down, Jess, I—"

"As a matter of fact," Jessica interjected, "it seems to me I actually did you a favor today.

Didn't I help you get a handle on how to deal with Todd?"

"In your own way I suppose you did," Elizabeth answered.

"So can't you help me out now with this itty-bitty favor?"

Elizabeth knew she was being manipulated, but she was in no mood to challenge her sister. "OK, I'll ask her," Elizabeth said, "but don't be surprised if she says no."

"I know you'll do your best, Liz," Jessica said, once again full of her usual confidence. "You always do."

The following morning Enid caught up with Elizabeth at the bus stop. "Heard I missed a lot of excitement yesterday," she said, her bright green eyes sparkling as she spoke.

"The grand reopening? All you missed were free T-shirts and greasy food."

"And what about that super rescue by our hero Todd Wilkins?"

"Well, it wasn't exactly heroic. He just happened to come along at the right time."

"Gee, I'd think you'd be the first one to be singing his praises."

Elizabeth caught her breath. She didn't know why she was putting Todd down this morning. Ordinarily she'd have made a big deal out of the event in the Dairi Burger parking lot. Was she, despite her better judgment, letting the motorcycle influence her feelings about Todd after all?

It was better not to think about it. "Oh, by the way," she began, changing the subject, "how are the party plans coming along?"

Enid rolled her eyes heavenward. "Liz, my mother's really starting to go wacko over this affair. First the engraved invitations, now it's the food. Last night she was threatening to fire the caterer. 'I'm not going to use a person whose idea of *haute cuisine* is pigs in blankets,' " Enid said, imitating her mother's nasal twang.

"Pigs in blankets don't sound so bad to me."

"Me either. But Mom insists on going first class all the way. It wouldn't surprise me if we ended up with caviar on toast points. Yech." She wrinkled her nose. "Well, at least I got the invitations made out. I even have one for you."

Elizabeth saw this as her opportunity to help out her sister. "Did you send one to your cousin Brian?" she asked, trying to sound as casual as she could.

Enid replied, "Didn't I tell you he was coming? He'll be in on the Friday before the party."

"I forgot," Elizabeth fibbed. "You know, I don't think I've seen him since the summer."

"That's because he hasn't been here since then."

"Is he still as cute as I remember?" Elizabeth went on. Jessica would certainly want to know.

"Cuter," Enid noted. "He's been working out with weights. He's really started to fill out."

"I'll bet you can't wait till he gets here."

"You'd better believe it. Besides you, he's the only one I can complain to about Mom." She did a double take. "Hey, why the sudden interest in Brian? You want me to fix him up with somebody?"

With the matter put so bluntly before her, Elizabeth felt her confidence slipping. Maybe now wasn't such a good time to try to sell Enid on Jessica, Elizabeth thought. "I just think Brian's a great guy. I'm glad he'll be in town," she said weakly.

"I'll tell him you said that." Enid was sure there was more to it than that, but she didn't push her friend. "Now, tell me how Todd clobbered Crunch McAllister."

"He didn't clobber him. All he did was let Crunch ride his Yamaha."

"It must have been a sight."

"It was." But the sight Elizabeth recalled was the one of Mandy holding on tightly to Todd's waist.

"Well, how do you like that? Here's the great man now," Enid announced, looking up the street.

Elizabeth felt her stomach tighten as she turned to see Todd approaching on the bike. About a block away he cut the engine and rolled along the curb silently until he reached the bus stop.

To reassure herself of her feelings for him, Elizabeth walked up to him, unsnapped the visor on his helmet, and kissed him on the lips.

"Well, and a good morning to you, too," Todd said, removing his helmet. He got off the bike and hugged her. "I started to come up your street to pick you up when I suddenly realized I wasn't in my car. Stupid of me, huh? I guess old habits die hard."

"I'm glad you decided to stop here," Elizabeth said, returning the hug as hard as she could.

While the two of them continued to wrap themselves in each other's arms, Enid sorted through a thick stack of cream-colored envelopes she'd taken from her canvas carryall. She picked out two of them and held them up in the air.

"Hey, you lovebirds," she called out, "as long as I've got you together, I might as well give you these."

"What are they?" Todd asked, taking one of the envelopes Enid held out as Elizabeth did the same.

Enid giggled. "Open them."

Inside were the elegantly engraved invitations to her party, including separate RSVP cards. "Hey, pretty fancy. What are these made of, silk?" Todd asked.

"No, they're paper. But they cost about as much as silk. Big waste of hard-earned money, if you ask me."

"Your mom thinks you're worth it," Elizabeth said. "And so do I."

"Thanks, Liz. I feel the same way about you," Enid said, blushing. She cherished their friendship deeply and was glad to hear Elizabeth admit it, too. "So how about it, guys," she said lightly, switching to less personal matters. "You coming to the party?"

"Of course," Todd said. "Want my RSVP now?"

"You're good for it," Enid said with a wink.

"It's going to be a busy day for me," Todd continued. "My grandfather's having a birthday party the same day. But fortunately his party's in the afternoon, so I can make it to both."

"Well, I'm glad you can," Enid said sincerely and smiled.

"Hey, how'd you like a little prebirthday present, Enid?" he asked.

"Such as?"

"How about a ride?" he asked motioning toward the motorcycle parked behind him.

"You mean it?" she asked.

"A quickie. Just around the block."

"Great!" she shouted. "Liz, mind holding these?" She handed Elizabeth her books and her bag before hopping on the back of the bike.

As Elizabeth balanced the books in her arms, she heard Todd say, "Now, you can hold on to those arm rails, but I think you'll be more comfortable if you wrap your arms around my waist." And suddenly that same jealous feeling Elizabeth had experienced the day before came rushing over her.

A second later Enid and Todd were off, shooting down the street like a miniature space shuttle.

Elizabeth crooked her head in the opposite direction, looking for signs of the school bus. She wished it would hurry and get there and carry her away from this spot and the whole horrible situation. Every shift of gears on Todd's bike sent a surge of confusion and anguish through her. *It's not fair*, she cried to herself. *Why can't I accept the sight of another girl on Todd's bike?*

Less than two minutes later the bright yellow school bus edged up to her corner. But the relief she expected to feel at its arrival was tempered by the fact that Todd had not yet returned with Enid. What was taking them so long? She hesitated before stepping onto the bus, uneasy about leaving without Enid. But then she realized that when the two of them returned and saw she was gone, they would figure out what had happened.

For the second day in a row, her friends would see the backseat of Todd's bike occupied by another girl. The thought made the french toast she'd had for breakfast sit even more heavily in her stomach.

Blinking back tears, she found a seat on the bus and rode to school alone.

Five

Elizabeth didn't know how much longer she could take it. It was only Todd's second day on the bike, and already she was imagining that every girl he rode with was a candidate to take her place. Even Enid, the last person in the world who'd ever want to steal Todd, seemed a threat.

The tension she'd felt at the bus stop had remained with Elizabeth through her stiff encounter with Enid at her locker. Enid had run up to her, her hair flattened by the helmet, her cheeks flushed with excitement. It was clear to Elizabeth that her friend had enjoyed herself—

and she was in no mood to hear about it. Silently she'd handed Enid her books and run off. She hadn't meant to be so abrupt, but she couldn't help it. She only hoped that Enid would understand and wouldn't be offended.

Elizabeth continued to be preoccupied through all of chemistry, where she tried unsuccessfully to focus on Mr. Russo's lecture on oxidation, and then through Ms. Dalton's discussion of the verb *savoir* in French class.

She was happy when the bell rang, signaling the end of class. Next was a study period, and today that meant work on her newspaper column. Perhaps it would help take her mind off Todd. In a kind of daze she threaded her way through the crowded halls toward the newspaper office. Had she turned her head just the slightest bit or stopped to say hello to a friend, she might not have looked through the big glass doors of the library and seen what she did. She wouldn't have seen Todd sitting at a table—with Mandy Farmer snuggled up beside him, her arms resting on his shoulder as they pored over a book.

At that moment Elizabeth wished she were Jessica. Her sister would have taken in the scene and strode through the doors with a grin, given Todd a kiss, and breezily asked how things were going in the whale-saving game.

And everyone in the room would have looked

at them, and Mandy Farmer would have thought twice about sitting so close to Todd.

But Elizabeth wasn't Jessica, and instead of going into the library, she continued down the hall, trying to pretend that what she had seen didn't matter.

The *Oracle* office was empty except for Mr. Collins, faculty adviser of the paper, and one of Sweet Valley High's favorite teachers. Elizabeth smiled back as he looked up from the layouts he was examining and flashed her a welcoming grin. She thought the strawberry-blond teacher looked especially handsome in the blue crewneck sweater he wore with jeans and a tweed jacket. It wasn't hard to see why practically every girl in school had had a crush on him at one time or another.

"In to work on your column?" he asked.

"I'm going to write it now," Elizabeth said, taking a seat behind one of the ancient typewriters. Trying to look as carefree as possible, she tossed her golden ponytail to one side, rolled a piece of paper into the machine, and typed out "Eyes and Ears."

But nothing else came out. All she could think about was Todd—and that empty space on the back of his motorcycle.

Elizabeth didn't even know how long she'd been staring at the blank piece of paper when Mr. Collins came up behind her and rested a gentle hand on her shoulder. "Got a case of writer's block?"

She looked up at his concerned face. "I wish that were all," she said glumly.

Roger Collins pulled up a chair. "Do you want to talk about it?"

It was funny, Elizabeth thought. Mr. Collins was always around when she needed him. "I think I'd better, before the white coats come and take me away," she quipped. She pulled the paper out of the typewriter, crumpled it into a ball, and threw it toward the wastepaper basket halfway across the room. She missed.

"Come on, Liz," he said. "Whatever it is can't be that bad."

She shrugged. "In a way, nothing's wrong. But in another way, everything's wrong."

"The classic paradox," Mr. Collins mused, resting his hand on his chin. "I'm not sure I know what yours is about, but I'd be more than happy to listen if you want to explain it to me."

As if a dam had burst, the words began to rush from Elizabeth's mouth. She told Mr. Collins about Todd, the bike, and her inability to share it with him. She admitted her fear that Todd would lose interest in her because of it—and be attracted to someone who was as fond of two wheels as he was.

"Let me ask you a question," Mr. Collins said

after she had finished. "Todd's a basketball player, right?"

Elizabeth nodded.

"Do you think he's interested in dating anyone on the girls' basketball team?"

Elizabeth shook her head.

"And do you want to go out with every boy who shares your love of literature?"

"Of course not."

"But you feel he might be interested in Mandy or Enid because they enjoyed riding with him on his bike?"

"No, not when you put it that way," Elizabeth said, grinning slightly. "No, I guess not."

"Do you think it's wrong for them to ride with Todd?"

"No, I'm sure it's a lot of fun for them," she said. "But you see, Mr. Collins, that's what's getting to me. I *know* there's nothing wrong with what they're doing. Yet it's got me upset anyway. And I hate feeling this way."

Mr. Collins grew silent, his blue eyes watching her in a way that was friendly and reassuring.

"Well?" she asked softly. "Am I going nuts or what?"

"Not at all. Matter of fact, I think your reactions prove you're a normal, healthy girl."

That wasn't the answer Elizabeth expected. "That's terrific," she said, throwing her hands in the air in frustration. "I can't make sense out of what's going on in my life, and you tell me there's nothing wrong."

"I didn't say everything was rosy. All I meant was that it's normal to have feelings of envy, jealousy, or even hatred. Every sensitive person I know has those feelings. And everyone's got to find out how to handle them. Believe me, Liz, you're not alone. Everyone has to deal with similar emotions at some time or other." He paused to let the words sink in.

Elizabeth didn't have to ask what he was talking about. She was well aware of the divorce Mr. Collins had gone through and how his encounters with his ex-wife regarding their son often left him emotionally drained. But he always managed to present a cheerful and sympathetic face to his students. Elizabeth decided to take her cue from him.

"So what do I do now, coach?" she joked.

"The important thing is not to deny your emotions. I'm sure you'll work everything out in time. You've got a firm grip on your values and a deep faith in yourself. Take it from me, those things will pull you through. But let me ask you—have you spoken to Todd about this?"

"Not about Mandy and the rides."

"Don't sell him short. I know Todd cares about you and wouldn't consciously do anything to hurt you. Maybe a talk with him is all you need to be yourself again."

Elizabeth conceded he might have a point. Todd had, after all, understood her reasons for not riding with him. "Thanks, Mr. Collins. I think you've helped me with my writer's block."

"Good," he said, winking, "because I want to see that gossip column by the end of the period. I'm dying to know what's going on around here."

With the burden lifted from her mind, Elizabeth tore into the column, leading off with the story of Todd's heroics in the Dairi Burger parking lot. She wrote another paragraph on the scene at the reopening, adding a brief line advising her readers to see how their first hot clam special went down before having seconds.

"Thanks again," she said, handing Mr. Collins her column. With people like him on her side, she felt she might get all the support she needed to help her sort out her feelings.

Elizabeth arrived at the cafeteria early. She had already gone through the line and claimed a table on the outdoor patio by the time Enid came around, her plate piled high with the day's main selection: rubbery-looking macaroni and cheese. She sat down across from Elizabeth, who had a faraway look on her face as she munched on a carrot stick.

"Everything OK?" Enid asked, concerned.

Elizabeth chewed and nodded.

Enid wasn't convinced. "Hey," she persisted, "you're not mad at me for riding with Todd, are you?"

"Of course not," Elizabeth replied.

"Are you sure?" Enid probed. "I don't know if you're aware of this, but this morning at the lockers you had icicles in your eyes. For a moment there I thought you were Jessica."

"I'm sorry, Enid. I didn't mean it," Elizabeth said sincerely. "I guess I was a little upset. But not really with you."

"I didn't think you'd mind. I'd never been on a motorcycle before, and I thought it'd be fun. It was just supposed to be a little ride. But then when I missed the bus and all—"

"Forget it, Enid," Elizabeth interrupted her. "No apology's necessary. Really. I'm glad you had a good time."

"I'd never know it to look at you."

"Don't mind me. I'm going through a rough time."

"Want to talk about it?"

"Maybe later," Elizabeth hedged.

A little embarrassed to look her friend in the eye, Elizabeth let her gaze wander. She spotted Jessica and Lila crossing the patio with their trays and suddenly remembered her sister's request about Brian. Jessica hadn't been too thrilled to learn she hadn't yet broached the subject with Enid. Elizabeth figured now was as good a time as any to ask about Brian. She was afraid that if she waited too long, Jessica might decide to take matters into her hands—and who knew what would happen then!

"Listen, Enid, I have a favor to ask."

"Sure, what is it?"

"Could you fix Brian up with Jessica at your party?" The words came out in a jumbled rush.

Enid chewed for the longest time before answering. "Liz, you know you're my best friend in the whole world," she stated, "but the answer is no."

"Why not?" Elizabeth asked, knowing full well why not, but hoping to convince Enid otherwise. After all, Brian would probably have a great time with her sister. What guy wouldn't?

"If it were anyone else, I'd say yes in an instant. But Jessica hurt me very deeply, Liz. I don't have to tell you. I still haven't forgiven her for it, especially since she's made it clear that I'm nothing more to her than a nuisance who hangs out with her sister."

"But, Enid," Elizabeth persisted, "you haven't even *thought* about Ronnie for months. And you and George are very happy now."

"That's not the point," Enid insisted. "Jessica never once said she was sorry. Why should I do her a favor? Besides, I thought she was interested in Danny Stauffer. Didn't you tell me he drove her to the Dairi Burger yesterday?"

"I don't think she takes him seriously," Elizabeth said.

"Then she doesn't need to play around with my cousin either. Sorry, Liz, the answer is still no."

Elizabeth was about to make one final pitch for Jessica when Todd rushed over and planted a hasty kiss on the top of her head.

"How are you doing, Todd?" Elizabeth asked.

"Frankly I'm a bit crazed," he said, catching his breath. "I just came over here to grab some food and let you know I can't meet you after lunch like I promised."

"The project?"

"What else?" He shrugged. "I'm really sorry, but Mandy's waiting for me in the library. She's probably neck deep in newspapers—which is where I should be. See you all later."

Enid watched as Todd walked away, his long legs taking him quickly across the spacious lawn to the main building. When she turned back, she noticed that Elizabeth looked upset.

"Hey, earth to Liz." Enid snapped her fingers in front of her friend, who'd taken on a faraway look again. "Anyone home?"

"Sorry, Enid."

"If I didn't know better, I'd swear you were jealous. I saw the way you tensed up when

59

Todd mentioned Mandy. Liz, it's only a school project."

Elizabeth sighed deeply. "It's the bike, Enid. Todd's motorcycle. It's really gotten to me."

"What do you mean?"

Now that Elizabeth had begun to talk about it, she was glad; she could use a sympathetic ear. "For starters, Enid, it's made me envious. Do you know why I was edgy with you when I gave you back your books this morning? I was jealous of you."

"Of me?" Enid's eyes grew wide. "Why?"

"Because you were sharing Todd in a way I never will," Elizabeth admitted.

"I knew something was going on. I'm sorry, Liz. If I'd known—"

Elizabeth stopped her. "You didn't do anything. Don't you see? I'm the one who's mixed up. I'm letting this bike come between Todd and me. A stupid piece of machinery—and it's causing me more grief than a busload of girls ever could."

Six

Guy Chesney caught up with Elizabeth by her locker after school. "Hey, Liz, how's my favorite newspaper reporter?"

Elizabeth looked into the friendly brown eyes of The Droids' keyboardist. "Fine," she said, giving him a smile.

"I just saw Todd, and he told me you're not riding with him. Thought you might like a lift to the Dairi Burger."

"Thanks, Guy. It sure beats taking the bus," Elizabeth replied.

Guy's grin brought out the dimple in his left cheek. "This way, my dear," he said, taking her by the arm and leading her down the nearly empty hall. "Here, let me take those," he added, gesturing toward the books resting in her other arm.

"That's all right, I can handle them," she said, declining the offer. "So how are things with The Droids?"

"Fine. I've been writing up a bunch of new songs, and if you ask me, I think Dana's voice is getting better and better."

"I'm glad you guys didn't decide to break up after the fiasco you had with that manager."

"As Max said, it just wasn't meant to be," Guy said philosophically, referring to the band's failed first attempt at stardom.

"That doesn't mean it won't ever happen," Elizabeth countered. "It's just going to take a little more time."

"By the way," Guy interjected. "I never really thanked you for the help you gave us, writing all those articles in *The Oracle* about us and everything."

"It was my pleasure," Elizabeth told him. "I wish I could have helped you more."

"That's all right. At least the experience proved that we aren't ready for the big time yet. But we will be one day soon, I'm sure of it."

They arrived at Guy's car, a late-model station wagon, its back filled with musical equipment. "You take your keyboards everyplace you go?" Elizabeth asked after Guy opened the passenger door for her.

"Never know when someone's going to need some music," Guy said, grinning. "Actually, I'm going over to Max's later, to practice. After I get a bite to eat."

Elizabeth marveled at the change in Guy since the last time she'd talked to him. He was so relaxed and confident, nothing like the tightly wound, nervous musician who was ready to explode anytime one of his group members hit a wrong note. "You're going to be playing at Enid's party, aren't you?" she asked.

Guy started up the car and steered out of the parking lot with his left hand while he rested his right arm on the top edge of the front seat. "That's our next gig. You going with Todd?"

"Of course," Elizabeth said, looking out the window as she spoke.

"Todd's sure a lucky guy," Guy remarked, "to have a girl like you."

"Thanks, Guy," Elizabeth said.

"I mean it. But could I ask you a question?"

"Sure."

"How come you're not riding with him?"

Elizabeth felt her stomach tighten again. He was only about the eighth person who'd asked her that question that day, and she was getting tired of explaining why. "Personal reasons," she said tersely.

Guy picked up on her uneasiness. "Doesn't sound like you're too happy about it."

Elizabeth sat straight. "It's nothing I can't handle, Guy."

"Well, I just want to let you know that anytime you need a ride, just say the word, and I'll be there." Guy let his arm slip a little, just enough so that it now rested on Elizabeth's shoulder.

She moved away. "That's sweet of you," she said, watching the scenery rush past her.

Stretching his arm as far as he could, Guy edged her back toward his side. "A closed car can be a lot more fun than a motorcycle," he hinted.

Elizabeth turned to face him, the signal he was sending quite obvious to her. "Thanks, but no thanks, Guy," she said, moving as close to the door as she could.

"I mean it, Liz. As a friend."

"*Just* as a friend, Guy. OK?" Elizabeth breathed a sigh of relief as, at that moment, they pulled into the Dairi Burger parking lot.

Todd was already there, leaning against his bike, waiting for her. "I've got to go," she said, turning back to Guy. "But thanks for the ride. See ya." Quickly she got out of the car and walked toward her boyfriend.

She saw Todd's smile begin to fade as she approached, with Guy following persistently, not too far behind her. "Hey, you forgot these," he said, catching up to her. He handed Elizabeth her books and added with a flirtatious wink, "Think about what I said, will you?"

"What was that all about?" Todd grumbled as the two of them went inside and approached the counter.

"Nothing," Elizabeth said, before ordering the hot clam special and a root beer.

"Why are you ordering that?" he whispered after ordering a cheeseburger and fries for himself. "It's awful."

"I want to give it one more chance. Maybe it's improved."

Neither one said another word until their food was ready and they had grabbed an empty table near the window. Then Todd spoke up.

"You still haven't explained what you were doing in Chesney's car."

"Nothing," she repeated. "He gave me a ride, that's all."

"Well, I don't like it," Todd muttered darkly, taking a bite of his burger.

"Don't like what?" Elizabeth asked, scooping up some of the clam mixture with her fork.

"You riding with another guy."

Elizabeth's eyes grew wide as an amazing revelation sunk in. "Todd Wilkins, I believe you're jealous."

"Darn right, I am!"

Without warning, Elizabeth began to laugh, loud enough so that some heads turned in the next booth.

"Would you mind telling me what's going on here?" Todd demanded, anger rising as Elizabeth's giggles continued.

She took a deep breath, then quieted down. "I'm sorry, Todd. It's just that you've made a light bulb go on in my head."

"Now I'm really confused."

"You've made me see how silly I've been acting for the past two days," she explained.

"About what?"

"That thing out there." She waved her fork in the direction of the parking lot.

"You mean my bike? I thought we cleared that up."

"I thought so, too, until I saw you riding with Mandy yesterday. And Enid this morning."

Todd looked hard at Elizabeth as he grasped the meaning of her words. "Are you trying to tell me you were jealous also?" Then he smiled as he realized they had been feeling the same way, without being aware of it. "Gosh, Liz, I thought you knew better," he said, breaking into a laugh that matched hers.

Elizabeth reached across the table and ruffled his hair playfully. "And I thought you knew better than to think I'd have something going with Guy. Which I don't," she added for emphasis. "All I did was catch a ride with him."

"I guess I knew that all along," Todd said. "But something inside me didn't like seeing you with him."

"And I guess I know that you meant nothing by giving Mandy a ride. But when I saw her holding on to you, I couldn't help but think that you liked that feeling—and that if I couldn't be on the back of your bike, then eventually you'd find someone who was more willing."

"Why didn't you tell me it bothered you so much?"

"I guess I was afraid of sounding too demanding."

"Well, you don't. And I don't ever want you to be afraid of talking to me about anything again. I'm glad you finally spoke up. Now that I know it bothers you, I won't offer any more rides to other girls."

"Todd, you don't have to—"

He shook his head emphatically. "It's what I want to do, not what I have to do. You're the only person I really want to ride with me, and if you can't, then nobody else will, either. I want to pretend you're on the bike with me every minute. From now on that empty seat's reserved—even if you can't use it, it still belongs to you."

"Thanks," Elizabeth said. "I couldn't ask for anything nicer."

"Anyway," Todd continued, "if you were worried about Mandy going after me, you can forget it." He pointed to one of the corner booths, where Mandy was sitting with Winston Egbert. They were seemingly lost in their own world, feeding each other french fries.

"When did that happen?" Elizabeth asked.

"They both discovered they have this thing about whales," Todd said, adding, "I'm sure going to be glad when this project we're working on is over. Having to watch the way those two act when they're together is beginning to get to me."

"And so is this clam special." Elizabeth smiled and tossed her fork down on her plate in playful disgust.

Seven

Elizabeth was doing her French homework when the phone rang that evening. Thinking it might be Todd, she dropped everything and picked it up on the second ring. It wasn't Todd, but it was for her.

"Hey, what's going on with you and Todd?" Enid asked her. "When I got to the Dairi Burger, you guys were huddled so close together I thought I'd be intruding."

"You could have joined us," Elizabeth said happily. "We were just celebrating the realization that Elizabeth Wakefield isn't going Loony-toons after all."

"That's a relief. For a while there I was getting really worried about you. Do you mean you're all sorted out on that bike business?"

"Yes. I've finally come to terms with it. It's only a means of getting from place A to place B. Nothing more, nothing less. And my not riding on it hasn't changed Todd's feelings about me one bit."

"That's terrific news," Enid responded. "But now on to another subject. Did you tell Jessica what I told you about Brian?"

"Yeah, when I got home. I can't say she took it too well. She hardly ate a thing during dinner."

"That's too bad," Enid fretted. "I've been doing a lot of thinking, and I've changed my mind. I've decided to fix up Jessica and Brian."

"You really mean it?" Elizabeth couldn't believe her ears. "That's great, Enid. Jess is going to love to hear that. But what made you reconsider?"

"I had a long talk with George about it, and he made me see how wrong it was to keep punishing her for what happened. 'Keep the past in the past', he told me. By turning her down, I was just being spiteful, and that's a pretty dumb thing to do—particularly since I know Brian would have a good time with her. I just called him to let him know what was going on, and he thinks it's a great idea. He had such a good time that day we all spent at the beach last summer. He can't wait to see her again."

"And I can't wait to tell her," Elizabeth bubbled.

"I hope you can wait a couple of minutes," Enid interrupted, " 'cause there's something else on my mind. My mother."

"More party stuff?"

"It's getting worse by the minute, Liz. She's thrown herself into every little detail—the flowers, the decorations, even the little party favors. It's all she cares about nowadays. And it all means so little to me."

"I know," Elizabeth commiserated.

"I almost get the feeling . . ."

"What?" Elizabeth probed.

"It's almost as if the party is more important to her than I am. No, that's not exactly what I mean. More like it's starting to be *her* party. Does that sound crazy to you?"

"I know what you're saying, Enid, but if I were you I'd try to enjoy it. She's probably just having a good time making the preparations."

"You really think so?"

"Well, the party was her suggestion, so she was under no obligation to make it this elaborate. Face it, Enid, she's doing it because she loves you."

"After all that grief I put her through, I'm not sure why." Enid winced, remembering the days when the problems in her family had driven her to join a wild crowd and get heavily involved with drugs.

"That's the point, Enid. You came pretty close to hitting rock bottom at one point, but you survived. You're doing great now. I think your mom is pretty proud that you've made it to sixteen in one piece. For a while there she probably didn't think you were going to make it at all. This party is a celebration for her as much as for you."

"When you put it that way, I see what you mean. She probably *is* throwing this party out of love for me. If she wants to make a big deal out of it, I guess I have no right to stop her."

"That's the idea."

"But I refuse to make myself crazy over it, too!" she added emphatically. "Gosh, Liz, do you think I really care whether there are yellow or blue carnations on the tables?"

"No," Elizabeth said, chuckling. "Look, I've got to go. I think Jessica's in her room, and I want to give her the good news. See you tomorrow. 'Bye."

Elizabeth hung up the phone and scurried off to find her sister. She didn't have to go far. Jessica was standing before the mirror in the bathroom the two girls shared, brushing out her long blond hair. "I never should have tried that new shampoo," Jessica said, noticing Elizabeth's reflection. "It's made my hair so lifeless."

"You can use mine," Elizabeth offered. "Especially the night of Enid's party. I know you'll want to look great for your date with Brian."

Throwing down the hairbrush, Jessica whirled around and grabbed her sister by the arms. "Are you kidding? You mean Enid changed her mind?"

"She decided 'twas better to forgive and forget," Elizabeth said.

"I knew that girl would come to her senses," Jessica proclaimed. "Want to come help me pick out an outfit to wear? I can't be seen in just any old thing with Brian." She breezed into her room and yanked open her closet door.

The empty hangers on the rack were more a reflection of Jessica's disdain for orderliness than a lack of clothing. At least half her wardrobe was strewn in all corners of the closet, over and under the mismatched shoes that had been accumulating ever since junior high. Most of the rest of it was draped across the chair in the corner near her bed. Elizabeth couldn't see how Jessica ever found anything.

The truth was she didn't. "Darn, there's nothing here," Jessica grumbled, sorting through the few garments still hanging. "Oh, I just remembered." She stopped what she was doing. "I'd better call Danny while I'm thinking of it."

"What for?"

"To tell him I can't go with him to Enid's party."

"You were going to go with him?"

"I had to have someone to go with, and the party's less than two weeks away. When you told me Enid had said no about Brian, I called Danny."

"But I thought after the other day you didn't want to have anything to do with him anymore."

"Did I say that? I'll admit I wasn't wild about the way he handled himself with Crunch, but I suppose even Bruce Patman wouldn't have done well against that big brute. . . . Listen, did I tell you that Lila told me Bruce has been asking about me again?"

Detecting a note of excitement in Jessica's voice, Elizabeth said worriedly, "I didn't know you cared."

"Oh, I don't, Liz. I just find it very amusing."

Elizabeth wasn't so sure that was all there was to it. After the shabby way Bruce had treated Jessica during their intense but brief relationship, Elizabeth assumed her sister would never want to have anything to do with him for the rest of her life. But perhaps the torch Jessica had always carried for Bruce hadn't been totally extinguished.

However, that had nothing to do with the problem at hand. "What are you going to do about Danny?"

"Him? Oh, I'll think of something. I always do, don't I?" Jessica said sweetly as she did a quick inventory of the garments on the left side of her closet. "I've got it!" she announced.

"A dress?"

"No, a date for Danny. I remember overhearing Julie Porter say she didn't have a date. They'll love each other," she added before announcing, "I can't find a thing here, Liz. Maybe there's something in your closet?"

"Sure, let's go see," Elizabeth said generously, feeling happier than she had for days. "You know that green polka-dot dress with the puff sleeves? I think it would look terrific on you."

At that moment Elizabeth wouldn't have minded if Jessica wiped out her entire closet. For a day that had gotten off to a bad start, things were working out wonderfully for everybody now. Enid had George and her fancy party. Mandy had Winston. And now Jessica had Brian.

And she was more secure than ever in the knowledge that she was Todd's one and only girl.

Enid's party was going to be great, Elizabeth thought. She could hardly wait.

Eight

The Sweet Valley Country Club never looked better, Elizabeth decided as she entered the elaborately decorated ballroom in the club's main building, accompanied by Jessica and Brian. Enid's mother had really gone all out, turning the stately old room into a garden of multicolored flowers and plants. Every table had its own vase filled with blue and yellow carnations— Enid's compromise—and above the bandstand at the far corner of the room there was a huge floral arrangement that spelled out, "Happy Sweet Sixteen, Enid."

"Isn't it beautiful?" Elizabeth exclaimed.

"They've gone a little overboard on the flowers," Jessica chided.

"My aunt loves flowers," Brian noted. "Looks fine to me."

"But they *are* pretty," Jessica quickly added, not wanting to get off on the wrong foot with the guy she considered a monument to male perfection.

"Not as pretty as you," Brian whispered.

It was an old line, but Elizabeth felt that in Jessica's case it happened to be true. After much searching, her twin had finally found an outfit that did her justice, a black-and-white satin jumpsuit held in place by two tiny spaghetti straps. With her hair piled atop her head and long black-and-white earrings dangling from her lobes, Jessica looked stunning.

Brian was a fitting companion, his six-foot-plus body shown off by the Egyptian cotton dress shirt and charcoal-gray pants he wore. He was even more handsome than Elizabeth had remembered, and she planned to thank Enid for having changed her mind about Jessica. She only hoped that Jessica would show the same consideration.

"Why don't we see what they've got to eat?" Brian suggested, pointing to the table of gleaming silver chafing dishes straight ahead of them.

"Fine with me. Liz?" Jessica asked perfunctorily.

Elizabeth could tell from Jessica's tone that she wanted to be left alone with her date. "I'll stay here," she said, adding, "Todd ought to be along any second now."

"OK. And don't worry—Brian and I will take you to the club later." After a little prodding Elizabeth had convinced Jessica to give her a ride to the Caravan, Sweet Valley's newest rock club, where Enid planned to move the party after midnight.

"Though I can't understand why Todd couldn't borrow a car for tonight," Jessica needled.

"Don't start that again," Elizabeth warned.

"You're right. We're here to have fun. See you later."

Because the night was warm and clear and she felt a little awkward standing around alone, Elizabeth waited for Todd in front of the building, between the club's stately carved pillars. It was as good a place as any to survey the scene. Nearly everyone from school was beginning to arrive: Cara Walker and Ken Matthews, John Pfeifer, Winston and Mandy, Caroline Pearce, Penny Ayala, Lila Fowler and her date Tom McKay, Bruce and the brunette from the Dairi Burger. More of her friends were already inside, either dancing to The Droids' music or sampling the food.

After a while, Elizabeth wandered back into the ballroom. On her way over to the buffet table, she ran into Enid, who looked adorable in the teal-blue dress Elizabeth had helped her pick out the week before. George was at her side, his sparkling eyes reflecting the joy he took in watching Enid have her night in the spotlight.

"I've been looking all over for you," Enid declared. "When I saw Jessica come in without you, I began to get worried. Where's Todd?"

"Not here yet," Elizabeth said. "He had that party at his grandfather's, remember? It must be running late." What she left unsaid was her concern that something must have happened to Todd on his way there.

"Well, don't just stand around. Go check out the food." Enid blew a kiss into the air. "Worth every cent Mom spent."

"Any caviar?"

"No, but there are these great little shrimps and these cheese things that are just fantastic. You've got to try them," she said excitedly. "There are even pigs in blankets after all."

Elizabeth smiled. "You're glad she did it now, aren't you?"

Enid shuffled her feet. "Yeah," she admitted. "It is kind of nice."

Elizabeth peered into the crowd. "Hey, is that Mr. Collins I see over there?"

"Your eyes do not deceive you. Mom has to oversee the cleanup before going down to the Caravan, and he agreed to be our chaperon there. He looks gorgeous, don't you think?" Enid said, giggling.

"I'm glad he's here. I need to talk to him, so if you'll excuse me, Enid," Elizabeth said, "I'll be back in a few minutes."

Wading her way to the end of the table, Elizabeth caught up with the handsome teacher as he finished filling his plate with hors d'oeuvres. "I owe you one," she said.

Mr. Collins looked up and smiled. "For curing you of writer's block the other day?"

"That—and a whole lot more. You helped me straighten out my brain."

"That's one of the main functions of a high school teacher, Liz," Mr. Collins noted. "I'm glad things worked out for you."

"I can't imagine them better," she said. "I'm so lucky to have Todd. He's really so understanding. I can't say enough about him." She dropped her voice into an almost conspiratorial whisper and added, "But don't tell him I said that."

"Don't worry. My lips are sealed forever."

Elizabeth had sampled everything at the banquet table and was roaming around the room nervously when the phone call from Todd arrived. As she'd suspected, his grandfather's party had run late. He also told her he had some things to do before heading for the country club.

Elizabeth felt much better after speaking to him, glad her fears about his safety were unwarranted. She began to wonder, though, if she'd ever stop worrying about the motorcycle, if she'd always automatically suspect the worst whenever Todd was late for something.

Filing all those worries in the back of her mind, she resolved to enjoy the party as best she could until he arrived. Winston and George helped her out by dancing with her, but as it grew closer to midnight and Todd still hadn't shown up, she found herself getting worried again, and then annoyed. She'd looked forward to Enid's party for weeks, and now Todd had blown a big hole in it by missing practically the whole thing. He hadn't even had the consideration to break the date in advance, and the more she thought about it, the more she realized that she was, in effect, being stood up. Why would Todd do such a thing? she wondered angrily. After all they'd just gone through, it didn't make any sense. But, given the circumstances, all she could conclude was that he was avoiding her.

At a quarter to twelve couples began to filter out of the club for the trip downtown to the Caravan.

"Want a ride?" Enid asked as she and George were leaving.

"I'm going with Jess," Elizabeth told her, even though she hadn't seen her sister in over an hour. "She'll be back soon. And if worse comes to worst, your mom's offered to give me a lift after the cleanup."

Less than five minutes later Mrs. Rollins tapped Elizabeth's shoulder. "A young man is on the phone for you, Liz."

She rushed down the short flight of stairs to the pay phone just outside the women's lounge. "Todd Wilkins, where are you?"

"I'm really sorry, Liz," he said. "But it was something I had to do."

"What was, Todd?" she snapped. "Missing the party?"

"No," he answered, ignoring her icy tone. "I'll tell you when I see you. It's a surprise." Clearly he was enjoying his mystery.

"Todd, tell me now!" Elizabeth demanded. "What have you been doing all night?"

"I'll be up there in a few minutes. 'Bye."

Todd hung up before Elizabeth had a chance to ask him if he knew the party was moving to the Caravan. She would have liked to tell him to meet her there—where she'd have plenty of time to give him a piece of her mind.

The last remaining couples left for the club. Taking advantage of the balmy, moonlit night,

Elizabeth waited outside for the second time that night. This time, however, the wait was a short one. Less than ten minutes after he called, Todd pulled up on his motorcycle. "Everyone gone?" he asked, taking off his helmet and noting the silent and darkened ballroom windows.

"Jessica's coming back for me," Elizabeth began to explain. "She took off with Brian, and I'm waiting for her to—"

"She's got Brian to herself, and you expect her to come back here for you?" Todd interrupted.

Elizabeth shrugged.

Todd smiled wryly. "Well, I guess this is as good a time as any," he said.

"For what?"

Todd grew serious. "I've made another decision about us. And the bike." He patted the bike's gas tank, which gleamed in the moonlight. "It's the most difficult decision I've ever had to make, but it's something I have to do."

Elizabeth felt sick. Her anger at Todd dissipated as a sobering, dark thought set in. Todd's missing the party had nothing to do with his grandfather or with traffic. The "things" he'd had to take care of definitely had something to do with her. He sounded so solemn, she had the awful feeling she'd drawn the short straw in his choice between her and the motorcycle.

This wasn't the way it was supposed to be. Didn't the tender kisses they'd shared and the promises of love they'd exchanged mean anything to him? "Go on, Todd, get it over with," she said glumly.

"I know you're not expecting this—"

"Just say it, Todd, will you?" she pleaded, her eyes brimming with tears.

"OK." he announced with finality. "I'm selling my bike."

"What?"

"I'm getting rid of it—and don't try to change my mind," he insisted. "That's where I've been all this time. I made a deal with Crunch McAllister. I would have been here sooner, but he insisted on celebrating. Kept pouring me sodas while he chugged beer. Boy, can that guy drink."

Elizabeth didn't say a word. She began to cry.

"What did I say?" Todd asked as he enveloped her in his arms. With his index finger he tenderly wiped away her tears as a few began to form in his own eyes. He hated to see her cry. But what he didn't realize was that Elizabeth was shedding tears of joy.

"Why are you doing it?" she asked.

"I can't stand having to meet you places, and I can't stand watching you go home with other people—not to mention having to depend on that sister of yours. It just isn't worth it. We belong together, and if the backseat of the bike isn't your style, then it's up to me to make other arrangements."

"You mean you're doing it just for me? But what about your dream?"

"Dreams have a way of turning sour when they become real. It's funny, though. I'd wanted a motorcycle ever since I was old enough to know what one was. I worked hard for this baby—I don't have to tell you, it was supposed to be the best thing that ever happened to me. But you know what?"

Elizabeth drew back just far enough to see the tears in his eyes. "What?" she asked in a whisper.

"The best thing that ever happened to me is you. You mean more to me than any dumb piece of machinery. I couldn't stand the thought of losing you, and I couldn't see you tolerating this bike too much longer."

"Oh, Todd, I love you so much," she said, hugging him close.

"I love you, too," he said.

"Liz?" Their moment of intimacy was interrupted by the call from Enid's mother from inside the building. "I'm terribly sorry, dear, but I'm going to be tied up here for quite a while. I won't be going to the Caravan after all.

Shall I call a cab for you, or shall I tell one of your friends to come pick you up?"

Elizabeth looked at Todd and took in the love she saw in his eyes. Then she peered at the black metal shape parked just outside the door. Soon it would no longer be a part of Todd's life. Or hers. Suddenly it didn't look so menacing anymore. For the first time since Todd had bought the bike, Elizabeth pictured herself on the back of it, the wind whipping through her hair, her arms wound tightly around her boyfriend. Just once. Enid had thought her ride was lots of fun—and perfectly safe. Todd always handled the bike with care, and this was an opportunity for Elizabeth to see what it was like for herself, probably the only one she'd ever have. Could she? she wondered. Would she dare?

"No, that's all right, Mrs. Rollins," she said, making her decision then and there. "Todd will take me. And thanks for a great party."

Enid's mother smiled. "OK, Elizabeth. And good night to you both," she said, going back inside.

Todd drew Elizabeth closer again. "Liz, why did you tell her that?" When she didn't answer right away, he followed her glance to the Yamaha. "No, Liz," he said, reading her thoughts. "You don't really mean it. And even if you do, I won't let you."

Taking his hand, she walked him outside. "I want to," she said seriously.

"No, Liz. What about your parents?"

"What about them?" she replied with unusual petulance. "We're both making sacrifices because of them. I'm giving up the experience of riding that bike with you. And you're giving up your dream."

"But I made them a promise. I swore I'd never make you ride with me."

"You're not making me, Todd. It's something I want to do. Just tonight. And never again. Just once I want to feel what it's like to ride with you."

"But what about the promise you made to your parents?"

"They'll never have to know. Come on, let me ride with you. It's important to me, Todd."

"But I don't even have a helmet for you. Once I decided I wasn't going to give rides anymore, I figured I didn't need it. It's at home."

"We're not going very far. I won't need it just this once, will I?" she pleaded.

"But you're wearing a dress!"

"So what?" she replied. "Mandy was wearing a skirt when you took her. I'll be all right."

"I don't like this, Liz. . . ."

"I take full responsibility, Todd. Besides, deep

87

down I know it's what you want, too. Let's do it."

Elizabeth's joyous determination finally wore Todd down and helped him overcome his doubts. "You really want to do this?"

"Yes!" she exclaimed.

Todd began to smile. His fondest wish was finally coming true. Maybe it would be only this one ride, but he was going to do his best to make it an experience Elizabeth never forgot. "It's going to be great, Liz," he said. Enthusiastically he grabbed her by the waist and twirled her around in a circle.

"Ready whenever you are," she told him.

Playfully he bowed and pointed the way to the motorcycle. "My chariot, mademoiselle."

She answered with a curtsy. "With pleasure, *mon cher*."

"On second thought, let me go first," Todd said. He straddled the motorcycle and steadied it with his legs. "I want this thing to be perfectly level when you get on it." After he zipped up his jacket and put on his helmet, he turned to her and asked, "Ready?"

Elizabeth nodded, feeling a combination of anxiety and excitement, with a little bit of relief mixed in.

"OK, now hop on the back and rest your feet on those little pegs behind my heels."

Elizabeth did as he said and then wrapped

her dress around her legs. "Where do I put my arms?" she asked coyly.

"I thought you knew the answer to that," he said. "Just hang on to me as tightly as you can."

"Like this?" she said, clasping her arms around his waist.

"Perfect," Todd shouted. "Here we go!"

He pressed the starter button, and the engine roared to life. Slowly Todd turned down the club's long driveway, his eyes glued to the road ahead of him.

The first few seconds were the most frightening moments Elizabeth had ever experienced, even scarier than her first ride on the giant roller coaster at Magic Mountain. Trying hard to keep from shaking, she hung on to Todd for dear life, every muscle in her body tight as a drum. When Todd began to lean the bike first to the left, then to the right as they wound down the road from the country club, Elizabeth closed her eyes and held her breath, certain she was going to fall at any moment. She was beginning to regret having been so insistent about taking this ride.

But after they'd negotiated the curves and had begun the straight descent toward town, she opened her eyes again. Now that she saw she wasn't going to fall off, she started to relax and enjoy the ride. By the time they came to the next curves, she felt comfortable enough to lean into the turns with Todd, their bodies swaying together with the machine to create one streamlined entity. When they completed those turns successfully, Elizabeth felt remarkably exhilarated, as if she'd conquered Mount Everest.

And in a way she had. She'd conquered her fears.

The rest of the ride was like nothing Elizabeth had ever imagined. Even at Todd's careful speed, the evening air tickled her bare skin and tossed her long hair every which way. With her hands clasped tightly around Todd, she rested her cheek on his back and listened to her heart beat more loudly than anything around her. She relished the sensation of flying through the fresh night air. At last she finally realized what Todd was talking about when he referred to the thrill of being surrounded by the elements. She didn't want the ride to end.

When they got to the club, she was going to insist he keep the bike. That night when she got home, she thought, or better yet tomorrow morning when everyone was fresh and wide awake, she'd sit down with her parents and carefully explain why it was time for them to rethink their rule. There was nothing wrong with a motorcycle, she was going to tell them, not when it was being handled by someone as competent as Todd.

She closed her eyes and imagined that she and Todd were one person now, alone in space, whizzing through the wind. Nothing could stop them now. Nothing . . .

Nine

It was a fine time to think about Elizabeth.

Her body pressed tightly against Brian's, Jessica was caught in the ecstasy of one of the most thrilling kisses she'd ever experienced, when a picture of her sister entered her mind. It was as if she heard Elizabeth calling her. She wanted something, Jessica thought. But what? The sensation continued to niggle at Jessica even though she sought to shake it off and enjoy the intimate moment in the backseat of Brian's car.

Finally she remembered what she was supposed to have done. "Oh, no!" she cried, moving suddenly away from Brian.

Brian used his muscular arms to pull Jessica close to him again. "Hey, what's the matter?" he whispered.

But Jessica straightened herself up and adjusted the straps on her jumpsuit. "I forgot about Liz," she told him. "I was supposed to pick her up. What time is it, Brian?" she asked frantically.

"What did you say?" He nibbled on her ear, too caught up in his own enjoyment to hear her words.

Seeing how reluctant he was to help her, Jessica pulled back his shirt-sleeve herself and checked the time on his watch. "Twelve-twenty," she said aloud. "We should have gotten her a half hour ago."

"Don't sweat it," Brian told her, rubbing her arm gently. "I'm sure she's found another ride by now."

Jessica thought about it for a moment while she turned back to gaze at Brian. He sure was gorgeous, she mused, and his time at UCLA had certainly taught him a thing or two about pleasing girls. The thought of leaving his arms now distressed her to no end. "You really think so?" she asked Brian, wanting to be convinced he was right.

He smiled assuredly. "I think your sister has enough sense to realize that if you haven't come back yet, you're not going to."

That was true, Jessica thought, convincing herself that Elizabeth knew enough not to wait for her. "Maybe I was just overreacting," she told Brian. Running her fingers through his hair, her kisses showed him better than any words could that she was as reluctant to leave as he was.

Then why couldn't she get Elizabeth out of her mind? Something had to be wrong, Jessica concluded, an uneasy feeling sweeping through her body. She had the awful premonition that her twin was in trouble.

And she didn't think it had anything to do with being stranded at the country club.

Trying to hide her rising worry, Jessica eased out of Brian's grasp for the second time. "You're going to think I'm silly, Brian, but I can't stop thinking about Liz. If you don't mind, I'd like to stop by the Caravan and make sure she got there all right."

"I'm sure she did," Brian insisted.

"I'm sure you're right, too," she told him, "but I'd feel a lot better seeing for myself." Stroking his cheek with her fingertip, she added, "We wouldn't have to stay."

"Oh, all right." Brian sighed. "It wouldn't be much fun with you worrying anyway."

So they left Miller's Point and headed down the hill on the main road leading to town. About halfway there they noticed that, up ahead, the

94

darkened roadway was illuminated with the eerie red glow of traffic flares. Moving closer, they spotted the flashing red bubble lights of two Sweet Valley police cars.

"Looks like an accident," Brian said as he eased off the gas pedal.

"Must be a bad one, too. I think I hear an ambulance coming," Jessica noted.

Brian slowed to a crawl as they neared the accident site. "Look," he said, pointing to a purple van parked on the opposite side of the road. "Doesn't look damaged at all. Probably just a breakdown."

Jessica was just about to nod in agreement when she spotted the broken remains of a black motorcycle lying about a hundred feet beyond the van. "Oh my God!" she cried out when the awful realization sank in. "I think that's Todd's bike. Brian, we've got to stop!"

Jessica slumped in her seat as Brian eased off the road and parked. It looked bad. Todd was probably hurt. Or maybe even dead, she realized with a shudder. How was she going to tell Elizabeth?

Trying to fight down the feeling of dread within her, Jessica opened the car door and ran to the scene. But she was stopped by the firm hand of a female police officer. "You can't go in there," the officer insisted.

"It's OK," Jessica heard someone say. "She's her sister."

The words didn't register at first. From behind the police car came Todd, limping slightly, but otherwise appearing unhurt. "Todd, thank God you're alive!" Jessica cried, hugging him impulsively.

Todd seemed not to notice. As tears streamed down his face, he said, his voice cracking, "I tried to stop her . . . but she wouldn't listen."

Jessica pulled back, confused. "Todd, what are you talking about?"

"Liz. She . . ." Todd broke down.

"I think you'd better come with me, son." The officer took Todd by the shoulders and led him toward one of the ambulances that just had arrived.

It was then that Jessica saw her, her body lying twisted and motionless on the hard pavement. There were two policemen kneeling by her. "Liz!" Jessica screamed into the still night air. She ran as fast as she could across the empty roadway but was once again stopped, this time by a paramedic who'd gotten out of one of the ambulances.

"Liz!" Jessica shouted again, trying to free herself from the paramedic's grasp. But he dragged her a few feet away from the scene. "Let me go!" Jessica shouted hysterically. "That's my sister!"

At this point a policeman came over. "I'll take care of her," he said to the paramedic, who hurried over to Elizabeth's side.

When Jessica tried to run past the policeman, he blocked her way. He had to use all his strength to contain her, for she was kicking and clawing at him like a woman possessed. "Calm down," he told her. "Take it easy."

"Calm down? That's my sister!" Jessica cried again.

"We're doing all we can for her," the policeman told her. As he spoke, one of the paramedics was giving Elizabeth oxygen while another was already administering cardiopulmonary resuscitation.

"Oh, God! Is she going to die?" Jessica wailed, still struggling in the policeman's grasp.

"Not if we can help it. But you're going to have to calm down. You're not doing your sister any good by acting this way."

"But I have to see her!" Jessica demanded.

"As soon as her condition is stabilized, she'll be taken to the hospital. You can ride with her there."

Though she was still in a state of shock, Jessica heard enough of what the policeman said to realize that Elizabeth was still alive. That knowledge was enough to calm her down a little.

"I'll be all right now," she told him in her normal speaking voice. "Please let me go."

The policeman released her. Standing alone in the road, Jessica watched silently as the medical team worked feverishly on her sister. Brian came up to her then and put his arms on her shoulders, but she shook him off. She didn't want his comfort now. The only person she wanted to be with was Elizabeth.

Then a movement to the right of her caught her attention. It was a large figure being dragged away by two policemen. As he grew closer, Jessica could see his face clearly. It was Crunch McAllister, and as the realization of why he was there dawned on her, Jessica felt a hatred more intense than she had ever before known.

Before she knew what she was doing, she tore herself away from Brian and sprinted toward Crunch. He didn't see her coming until she threw herself on his alcohol-filled body and dug her pink fingernails deeply into his neck. The stale smell of beer stung her nostrils.

"Monster!" she rasped. "I'm going to make you pay for this!"

One of the policemen pulled her away, but while she was still within earshot, Crunch mumbled, "Todd was my buddy. I was gonna buy that bike, y'know. We made a deal. . . ." The rest of his words were lost as he sank into the backseat of the police car.

On rubbery legs Jessica walked back to the medical team as they were loading Elizabeth onto a stretcher. She waited until her sister was safely inside the ambulance before climbing in alongside her.

Jessica wasn't prepared to see her twin lying so limply under an oxygen mask, an IV tube taped to her pale arm. *My God, she looks dead.* Jessica thought, horrified.

"You're fine," she said aloud, cupping Elizabeth's left hand in hers. "She's going to be all right, isn't she?" Jessica asked the paramedic kneeling next to her.

Looking sad and tired, the man sighed deeply. "We're doing all we can. The rest is going to be up to her."

"Elizabeth Wakefield, listen to me!" Jessica cried. "It's me, Jess. You've had a little accident, and they're taking you to the hospital, but you're going to be all right. I just know you are. Do you hear me?"

Elizabeth continued to lie motionless, unresponsive to her sister's plea.

"Liz, you're going to get better," she said. "I'm going to make sure of it, you hear?"

But even as she said the words, Jessica had the horrible feeling that there was a very good chance she could be wrong.

Ten

Ned and Alice Wakefield arrived at the emergency room of Joshua Fowler Memorial Hospital shortly after receiving the call from the police. "Where's my daughter?" Ned Wakefield demanded of the nurse on duty.

The nurse looked up from her charts and said, "The doctor will be with you in a moment. Please have a seat." She pointed to the row of chairs alongside the yellow-tiled wall.

Neither of Elizabeth's parents felt like sitting. They paced back and forth in the small rectangular waiting room, weaving their way around ten other people sitting anxiously in their seats.

A short time later they were joined by their son Steven, who had left his dormitory room at college as soon as he'd heard the news.

"Any word yet?" he asked. His voice was hoarse from crying, but he tried to look as composed as he could.

"No," his mother said. "They're still working on her."

"Oh, Mom." Steven held his mother close. "She's going to be all right. Liz is a fighter. She'll never give up."

"I keep telling myself that, Steve."

His eyes scanned the room. "Where's Jessica? Does she know?"

"She's waiting outside the emergency room. On the phone the nurse told us she's been at Liz's side ever since the—the accident. She refused to stay out here in the waiting room."

All three looked up as the door to the waiting room opened and a lanky, youngish-looking man with a curly red beard came out. "Mr. and Mrs. Wakefield?" he asked, his eyes searching the room.

Steven joined his parents as they approached the doctor. "I'm Dr. Morales," he said, extending a hand to Ned Wakefield. "Chief of emergency medicine."

"How's my daughter?" Alice Wakefield burst out before he had a chance to say another word.

"Elizabeth's stable now, but her condition is serious. She's in a coma—"

The Wakefields all gasped. "Will she . . . ?" Ned Wakefield let his voice trail off, unable to utter the unthinkable.

"We don't know how serious it is and how long she'll remain in the coma," Dr. Morales continued. "The next twenty-four hours are going to be very critical."

"What are her chances?" Steven asked.

"Her vital signs are steady right now. She has a concussion and a few gashes on her legs, but she doesn't appear to have any major injuries. We're doing some tests now to see if we can measure the extent of brain damage."

"Just like Rexy," Alice Wakefield gasped, slumping against her husband.

"I don't want to alarm you," Dr. Morales went on. "It's quite possible your daughter can make a full recovery. But whenever someone receives a blow to the head, especially one as severe as the one she sustained, we can't rule out the possibility of brain damage. I just want you to be prepared."

"I want to see her," Elizabeth's mother said.

"Of course," said Dr. Morales. "We've moved her to the intensive-care unit. Her sister is with her now. You'll be able to see her soon. I'll have a nurse come and get you."

The Wakefields were too preoccupied to notice Todd's arrival. He took a seat in a corner of the room and waited quietly. After he'd been examined and released by the doctors, he'd made a few phone calls and then returned to await word on Elizabeth's condition. His father was with him. As soon as Dr. Morales left, Todd walked nervously up to the family.

"How is she?" he asked.

Ned Wakefield's worried face grew angry when he saw the boy. "She's alive for the moment—no thanks to you!" he shouted.

"You have every right to be angry at me, sir."

"Damn right I do. What on earth was she doing on that thing?" he rasped.

"You broke your word to us, Todd," Alice Wakefield said softly, but with an intensity that echoed her husband's.

Todd thought he had cried all he could, but now he was once again reminded of his terrible part in the tragedy. His eyes brimming with tears, he muffled a sob. "I know that, Mrs. Wakefield, and I'm sorry. You've got to believe that I never in my life wanted this to happen."

"It should have been you in there instead of her," Steven spat out with uncharacteristic bitterness.

"Don't you think I realize that?" Todd cried, the tears now flowing shamelessly down his cheeks. "Don't you think I've been telling myself the same thing, wishing I'd never let her on that motorcycle?"

"I think we'd better go now." Todd's father, Bert Wilkins, put his arm on his son's shoulder and led him away from the Wakefields. Returning briefly to the bereaved family, he said, "I'm very sorry. Our thoughts are with you."

Ned Wakefield nodded silently as Bert Wilkins walked back to his son. "Your mother's worried about you," he said. "Let's go home now."

"No, Dad. I want to stay here and wait."

"There's nothing you can do for Liz now, and under the circumstances I think the Wakefields would prefer to be alone. You can come back in the morning."

Picturing the look of hatred in Mr. Wakefield's eyes, Todd realized his father was right. His presence in the waiting room would do little to comfort them. But certainly the hospital was big enough for him to wait someplace else for word on his girlfriend. "No, I have to stay near her, Dad," he insisted. "I'll be all right."

Seeing the look of determination on Todd's face, Mr. Wilkins sighed and said, "OK. But call the minute you hear anything."

A few minutes later Mr. Collins, who had been notified by Todd about the accident, entered the waiting room, followed closely by Enid and George and more than a dozen of Elizabeth's friends, who'd left the party to see how she was. After consulting with the Wakefield family, Mr. Collins explained the situation to the kids, then urged them all to go home.

The last to leave was Enid, who hugged Elizabeth's mother and comforted her with the knowledge of how well her daughter was loved by everyone.

"I'll be back in the morning," Enid said, her mascara-streaked face showing her concern, "and if there's anything I can do for you, please let me know."

Mr. Collins stayed behind after everyone had left. He was as concerned about Elizabeth as anyone and sat down next to the Wakefields to await further word on her condition.

"You don't have to stay," Alice Wakefield told him.

"Your daughter's a very special person to me. I'd like to stay, if you don't mind."

"Of course I don't mind. I know Elizabeth would like it. She's spoken about you often."

"Is there anything I can get you, Mrs. Wakefield?" he asked. "Some coffee, perhaps? Or you, Mr. Wakefield? Steven?"

They were all touched by his kindness, but none of them could eat or drink anything. "Thank you, but not now," Mrs. Wakefield said. "Perhaps a bit later."

Mr. Collins rose. "If you'll excuse me, then,

I'm going to get myself a cup at one of the machines. I'll be back soon." Mr. and Mrs. Wakefield both nodded.

Mr. Collins followed the signs to the vending machines. As he walked into the corridor leading to the hospital's main wing, he found Todd, staring out of one of the big glass windows that overlooked the parking lot.

"You look like you need a friend," Mr. Collins said. When Todd didn't respond, he grabbed the boy around his waist. "Come on along with me," Mr. Collins said, leading him down the hall to the coffee machine.

Mr. Collins fished in his pocket for some change. "Want some?" he asked.

Todd shrugged. "I guess I could use it."

The teacher handed Todd a steaming cup of coffee. "Thanks for calling me tonight."

"I knew you'd want to know," Todd said miserably, joining Roger Collins at a nearby table.

"How are you feeling, Todd?"

"Under the circumstances, terrible. But I wasn't hurt, if that's what you mean. Just a few cuts. I just wish Liz . . ." He left the rest unsaid and looked down into his coffee.

"It must have been awful for you, Todd. Would you like to tell me what happened?"

Encouraged by Mr. Collins, Todd spoke about the accident for the first time. "It still seems so unreal." He shook his head, remembering the final moments before the crash. "We were coming down the hill—I was going slowly, taking my time, when all of a sudden I saw these huge headlights glaring at me. I tried to swerve and get out of the way—but it was too late." He pounded his fist on the edge of the table, coffee spilling over the edge of his Styrofoam cup. "The police told me Crunch was really loaded. I knew the guy had been downing beers all night, but I never thought he'd be stupid enough to take off in his van."

"You knew he'd been drinking?"

"Yeah, pretty ironic, wouldn't you say? The guy goes and smashes up the bike he's planning to buy. See, I agreed to sell him the bike, Mr. Collins. Tonight was going to be my last night on it. . . ." Todd took a deep breath, trying to contain the rage within him. "Oh, if only I'd put my foot down and said no to Liz. This would never have happened!"

Roger Collins was confused. "What do you mean?"

"Liz insisted on riding with me tonight," he revealed. "At first I thought it was a crazy thing for her to ask, but she really wanted to do it. Just once, she said to me. And I couldn't resist. The truth was, I didn't want to."

"And you blame yourself for that?"

He shook his head. "There's more. You see, I

promised her parents I'd never let her on that bike. But I thought no one would find out if I let her ride just once. I wanted to have her with me—but I should have said no."

"I don't think you did anything wrong," Mr. Collins said. "Liz knew what she was doing."

"I don't think she planned on it ending up this way."

"Of course she didn't, Todd. But what happened wasn't your fault. I'm sure the Wakefields agree, too."

"That's where you're wrong. They don't want to see me, Mr. Collins. That's their daughter lying in a coma. They hold me responsible as Crunch McAllister for what's happened. And I *am* responsible, Mr. Collins, no matter what you say!" Todd put his head in his hands, and his tears flowed again.

Mr. Collins rose and grabbed Todd by his shoulders. "Calm down, Todd. It was an accident, a cruel accident. I know you didn't want this to happen to Liz, and I'm sure, deep down, the Wakefields realize it, too. Don't blame yourself for something that couldn't have been prevented."

"But I could have refused to take her!"

"And leave her alone at the club? You didn't force her to go with you. It was something she chose to do. We both know how headstrong Liz can be when she makes up her mind to do something." He paused to consider his next words. "There's something else to keep in mind, too. Something Liz confided in me tonight. She has an enormous amount of faith in you. Do yourself a favor and don't let her down by torturing yourself with thoughts of what might have been."

"It's not easy."

"I know. Look—"

"There you are. My mother sent me to look for you." Steven Wakefield rushed into the room at full speed and ran up to Roger Collins. His voice shaking, he cried, "Liz has taken a turn for the worse. They don't think she's going to make it!"

Eleven

The strong yellow rays of the early-morning sun awakened Todd. For a split second he'd forgotten where he was and why he'd slept with his clothes on.

Then he remembered. The accident. And the horrible agony of the night before.

Todd had never been more scared in his life than in those agonizing hours when Elizabeth had hovered near death, when her life had been dependent upon the frightening-looking hospital equipment and the skill and persistence of the doctors. For a long time no one knew whether she'd survive the night. Nervously Todd had awaited the word on her condition from Roger Collins, who'd stayed with the Wakefield family through most of the crucial hours. He'd agreed that Todd should stay away from them for the time being.

After the doctors had finally gotten Elizabeth's condition stabilized again, Todd had given in to the fatigue he'd been fighting and he had curled up on an empty sofa in a second-floor lounge. Now that he was awake, though, he dashed quickly toward the intensive-care unit. There in the waiting room he found Ned and Alice Wakefield, their saddened eyes reflecting the strain of the all-night vigil. Hesitantly he approached them. He didn't care how they reacted to him now; he had to know.

"How is she?" he asked.

"The same," Ned Wakefield said wearily.

"But there's no brain damage, thank goodness," his wife added.

"Yes, the tests showed nothing wrong," Elizabeth's father continued. "But she's still in the coma."

"How long will she . . . ?"

As Ned Wakefield shrugged and shook his head, Steven entered the waiting area carrying a tray of food from the coffee shop. When he noticed his sister's boyfriend, all the emotions he'd been holding in check through the long night came bursting forth.

"What are you doing here?" he shouted. "I never want to see you again for as long as I live!"

"It was an accident, Steve."

"And it was all your fault!"

"My God, Steve, I love Liz. Do you think I wanted this to happen?" Todd cried.

"I don't know what to think. I mean, how am I supposed to feel when the doctors tell us how lucky Liz is to be alive—as if they call being hooked up to all those machines living. All I know is that you had no right to take her on that death machine. Look what you've done to her!"

"Stop it, Steve."

Everyone turned around as Jessica came out of the intensive-care unit. The stress of the ordeal showed clearly on her tired, heavy-lidded face. Her makeup was streaked, and her satin jumpsuit was heavily wrinkled from the night of sitting by her sister's bedside. But for once in her life Jessica couldn't care less about how she looked.

Her face was drawn tightly as she neared them. "If anyone's to blame, it's me," she said in an unusually quiet voice.

"Jessica, you don't know what you're saying," her father exclaimed.

"Yes, I do, Daddy. I didn't have the guts to tell you this last night, but the only reason Liz went with Todd was because I didn't pick her up as I promised. I thought I had more important things to do. . . ." She couldn't go on anymore as she was suddenly overtaken by the tears she'd been unable to shed until that moment.

"It's OK, honey." Alice reached over to comfort her sobbing daughter. "What's done is done."

"Nobody doubts your love for Liz, Jessica," Todd added. "And nobody blames you. The important thing is that we're all here. We all love her."

"I know you do, Todd," Jessica said, wiping her eyes. "During the night I remembered something Crunch said as the cops were taking him away. He told me he was going to buy your bike. You were selling it for Liz, weren't you?"

Todd nodded. "It was no fun without her. It wasn't worth it anymore."

"Todd, why didn't you tell us this last night?" Ned Wakefield asked.

"What good would it have done? We were all upset, and it would have sounded like I was making excuses."

"Roger Collins came to talk to us last night," Mr. Wakefield said. "He told us what happened. I know my daughter, Todd, and I don't think there's anything you could have done to keep her off that bike last night. I don't blame you for anything."

"Thanks, Mr. Wakefield," Todd said. "Unfortunately your forgiveness isn't going to make a difference to Liz."

Elizabeth's condition remained the same throughout the day. Except for the IV tubes in her arm and the respirator hissing by her side, she looked as if she were sleeping peacefully. Jessica spent as much time as the nurses would let her at Elizabeth's bedside, urging her, pleading with her to wake up. She talked incessantly about anything that came to mind. She told Elizabeth about the cheerful paintings in the hallway, about the equipment lining the walls of her room. She told her about the steady stream of friends who'd come by throughout the day to find out how she was.

"You've got to wake up, Liz," Jessica pleaded. "How can I live without you?"

Only the immediate family was permitted in Elizabeth's room, but that night Todd managed to sneak in. He joined Jessica at Elizabeth's bedside. He tried to be encouraging, but the demands of the day were finally taking their toll on Jessica.

"I overheard the doctor say that the longer

she stays like this, the worse her chances will be." Jessica's voice sounded dry as dust.

"She'll pull through." Todd took a chair and sat across the bed from Jessica. "She's got to."

Jessica shifted her haunted eyes away from Elizabeth to Todd. "You still think it's your fault, don't you?"

"I shouldn't have taken her, especially without a helmet. I should have known there'd be some drunken jerk on the road on a Saturday night. If it hadn't been Crunch, it could easily have been someone else."

"When I first saw her lying on the road, I was ready to kill you," Jessica confessed. "All I could think was that it was Rexy all over again. But as I sat there last night, I began to forget about that and see that I'm to blame, too. I think I knew I was going to leave her stranded at the club when I left. And I didn't care. Some sister I am."

"Jess," Todd said gently, "Liz knew you weren't going to pick her up."

"She did?"

"Your sister knows you very well, Jess. And if she wanted to, she could have found another way to get to the Caravan. But she had this crazy urge to get on the bike. After everything she'd ever said about it, I was surprised, believe me." He sighed wistfully. "It's funny. It was the kind of wild, spur-of-the-moment thing I

115

would have expected from you—but not from her."

"You're right, it doesn't sound like something Liz would ordinarily do. But I'll tell you this, Todd. There are going to be some changes around here. The minute she wakes up, I'm going to start making up for all the rotten things I've done to her."

"Jess, Liz loves you very much. I'm sure she doesn't think you've done—"

"I've done plenty," Jessica said, cutting him off. "I've really taken advantage of my twin, pretending to be Liz when it served my purposes, making her take the rap when I got into too much trouble to handle on my own. Remember that time she took the tour-guide test for me? I was too irresponsible to show up for that test myself. But do you think I thanked her?"

"I remember," Todd said. "She looked and acted so much like you she practically had *me* convinced."

"That's just the point, Todd. She's always doing things to please me—just because I'm her sister. I've thought about nothing else all day. She's been a better sister than I've deserved. I don't know what I'll do if she doesn't make it. She's just got to come out of this coma. She's got to!"

"That's why I came back just now," Todd

told her. "I'd like you to try something with me."

Jessica looked at him questioningly through tear-filled eyes.

"I was talking to Mr. Collins," he continued. "He told me that when he was around our age he had a friend who was in a coma. It was from doing drugs. The kid was in the hospital for days, and Mr. Collins and another friend tried this thing to bring him back. It sounded silly when he explained it, and there's no guarantee it'll work, but I think it's worth trying."

"I don't care what it is. I'll try anything to get my sister back."

Todd understood how deeply Jessica meant those words. He realized, perhaps more than anyone else, just how much of Jessica's spirit and soul were pinned to that bed. If Jessica lost Elizabeth, she wouldn't only lose a sister. She'd lose part of herself.

"Take her hand," he ordered.

She did, very gently cupping it in hers.

"Now take mine."

She extended her arm across the bed, and Todd grasped her cold, trembling fingers in his left hand. He gripped Elizabeth's fingers with his other hand.

"Squeeze," Todd said. "Squeeze as hard as you can."

She did as he asked.

"Now, think of her as before. Think of how beautiful she looked last night and repeat over and over, 'Wake up, Liz.' "

Never before did Jessica wish as hard for something to come true. Believing in her heart that it was going to work, she did as Todd said and pleaded with her sister to wake up and join all the people who loved her and needed her.

Yet Elizabeth remained unresponsive, her eyes closed to the world around her.

Will Elizabeth live or die? Find out in Sweet Valley High #7, DEAR SISTER.

Other books in the
Sweet Valley High
series you may have missed:

☐ **#1 DOUBLE LOVE** Meet the Wakefield twins, Elizabeth and Jessica. They're both popular, smart, and gorgeous, but that's where the similarity ends. Elizabeth is friendly, outgoing, and sincere—nothing like her twin. As snobbish and conniving as she is charming and vivacious, Jessica thinks the whole world revolves around her. Trouble is, most of the time it does. Jessica always gets what she wants—at school, with friends, and especially with boys. Even Elizabeth, who is usually wise to her twin sister's ways, has a hard time saying no to her.

This time Jessica has her sights set on Todd Wilkins, handsome star of the basketball team—

the one boy Elizabeth really likes. Todd likes Elizabeth, too, until Jessica starts interfering. There's nothing she won't do—from intercepting Todd's phone calls to wangling a date with Todd for the big dance. She even comes close to ruining her sister's reputation by letting the police think she's Elizabeth when she's picked up with troublemaker Rick Andover. Elizabeth is heartsick. She doesn't want to lose Todd, but it looks like he's falling for Jessica. Or is he?

□ #2 SECRETS Beautiful and ruthless, Jessica Wakefield is determined to be chosen queen of the fall dance at Sweet Valley High. If she can win the contest, she's sure to win Bruce Patman, the most sought-after boy in school.

The only person standing in Jessica's way is Enid Rollins. When Jessica discovers the truth about Enid's past—a secret so shameful Enid is terrified at the thought of anyone finding out— she knows the crown is within her grasp. She doesn't care that Enid is her twin sister Elizabeth's best friend—or that revealing the secret may cost Enid both her reputation and the boy she loves.

When Jessica lets the cat out of the bag— anonymously, of course—Enid is doubly stricken. Elizabeth was the only one who knew, she thinks; it must have been Elizabeth who betrayed her! Can Elizabeth convince Enid it wasn't her fault? Or will her scheming twin once again get away with murder?

□ **#3 PLAYING WITH FIRE** Watch out, Sweet Valley High! Jessica Wakefield is at it again. This time Jessica proceeds to sink her hooks into rich, handsome Bruce Patman, the most sophisticated guy at Sweet Valley High.

Or is it the other way around—has Bruce gotten his hooks into Jessica? Elizabeth notices a big change in her sister. In the past, Jessica had only to give a boy one of her dazzling smiles, and he would come running. Now suddenly she's following Bruce everywhere and dropping everything, including cheerleading, just to spend time with him.

Elizabeth doesn't trust Bruce one bit—he's arrogant, demanding, and way too fast. Jessica can usually hold her own with any guy, but this time Elizabeth's afraid her sister may be going too far.

□ **#4 POWER PLAY** Chubby Robin Wilson has been following Jessica around for months. First she wanted to be her friend—now she wants to join Pi Beta Alpha, Sweet Valley High's snobby sorority.

When Elizabeth nominates Robin for the sorority, Jessica is furious. Robin may be friendly and smart, but she's certainly not beautiful or popular enough to be a Pi Beta. Worst of all, she's fat. Jessica and her snobby friends are determined to find a way to keep Robin out.

But Elizabeth is just as determined to make Robin a sorority sister. Soon the twins are locked in a struggle that develops into the biggest power play at Sweet Valley High. But Robin has the biggest surprise of all in store for her enemies.

☐ **#5 ALL NIGHT LONG** Elizabeth Wakefield knows her beautiful twin can handle almost any guy—most boys are just no match for Jessica's seductive charms. But Scott Daniels, Jessica's latest love, is more of a man than a boy, much older and much more experienced than anyone Jessica's ever dated. He drives too fast, drinks too much, and doesn't like taking no for an answer—especially when it comes to girls.

When Jessica sneaks off to a college beach party with Scott, Elizabeth is afraid of what could happen. And when her twin isn't back by morning, Elizabeth's fears turn to alarm. Where's Jessica? Why has she stayed out all night?

Little does Elizabeth know she's once again about

to become a victim of her twin's irresponsibility. When Jessica doesn't show up at school in time for an important test, Elizabeth is torn between her own conscience and her desire to protect her sister—a choice that nearly costs her everything that's most important to her, including her boyfriend Todd.

A special bonus for fans of Sweet Valley High! Here's more about some of the people you've met in Sweet Valley and would like to know better.

One of the nicest teachers at Sweet Valley High is ROGER COLLINS. He's also the handsomest. With his strawberry-blond hair, gorgeous blue eyes, and athletic build, he could easily be a movie star. A lot of girls have crushes on him, but Mr. Collins knows how to handle those situations with grace and a sense of humor.

He teaches English. Also, he's the faculty adviser for *The Oracle*, for which Elizabeth Wakefield is a reporter and gossip columnist. Mr. Collins and Elizabeth are close friends. She goes to him for advice whenever something is really troubling her. She knows she can count on Mr. Collins to help her make the right decision without lecturing or judging her. He's that kind of person—easygoing, sensible, caring. He never treats her like a kid, either.

Roger has problems of his own, but he's careful to keep them to himself. A while back he went through a very messy, painful divorce. He loved May, his wife, but he couldn't ignore her wild behavior. She didn't even bother to hide it when she cheated on him. And often, he would arrive home to find May passed out in the bedroom next to an empty bottle of wine.

Roger was most concerned about their young son, Teddy, who is the dearest person in the world to him. He hated what all this was doing to Teddy. Also, he was afraid that one of these days, May's neglectfulness would cause Teddy harm.

After the divorce, May moved out of town, but she still came back once in a while to visit Teddy. She wanted Teddy to live with her, but Roger was firm on that subject: Teddy's safety came first. May took him to court, and it developed into a big custody battle. She pulled out all the stops, weeping on the witness stand and accusing Roger of trying to get back at her by robbing her of her child. In the end, the judge saw through her manipulations and awarded Roger custody.

Unfortunately, it didn't end there. Recently May took Teddy on one of her regular visitation days—but she didn't bring him back. Roger was frantic. He was sure his ex-wife had kidnapped their son. The police and Roger spent hours searching the area, but May and Teddy were nowhere to be found.

The next two days were like a nightmare. Roger phoned everyone he could think of who knew May and asked if they'd seen her. Finally, one of her friends broke down and confessed she knew where they were.

Roger raced over to the address, an apartment house in the next town. Teddy was there! Roger was so happy to see his son, he didn't even try to stop May as she crept out the back door.

It's been four months, and he hasn't seen May since. She still phones Teddy, but she's keeping her distance for the time being. Roger doesn't trust her, though. He's afraid she'd try it again if she ever got the chance.

Nevertheless, things are going well for Roger. For a long time after the divorce, he was too heartbroken to think about falling in love again. Lately, though, he's begun dating Nora Dalton, the pretty, raven-haired French teacher at Sweet Valley High. He thinks he could get serious— they always have a fantastic time when they go out—but he senses she's holding back in some way. Is there someone else? He knows she once dated George Fowler, one of the richest men in Sweet Valley, but that's over now. She's very secretive about her past, too. It's driving him crazy. What is she hiding? He can only hope she'll trust him enough one of these days to really open up to him.

Elizabeth suspects something is going on between Mr. Collins and Ms. Dalton, but she hasn't told Jessica. If Jessica knew, she wouldn't be so eager to baby-sit for Mr. Collins, on whom she's always had a semi-crush. And she wouldn't hesitate to break up that relationship by telling the entire school. Be careful, Mr. Collins!

COMING ATTRACTIONS

Scenes from the next episode of Sweet Valley High, *DEAR SISTER*

Jessica sat down slowly on the chair next to her sister's bed. Looking at the medical equipment, she shivered. She knew the IV tube going into Elizabeth's arm fed her sister life-sustaining nutrients. But the other tubes and machines frightened her.

Jessica took Elizabeth's limp hand in hers and pleaded, "Lizzie, you know how much I love you, how much everybody loves you. They love you more than me! You just can't die, Liz! I can't go through the rest of my life without you!"

Elizabeth's hand remained slack. There was

no answering squeeze, no flickering of eyelids. There was absolutely nothing.

A hand fell on Jessica's shoulder. Startled, she jerked her head up. Her blue-green eyes met a pair of soft brown ones in a kind face.

"Miss Wakefield?"

"Yes?"

"I could see the resemblance. You're both beautiful."

Jessica regarded the man in his white lab coat, afraid of the news he might bring.

"I can only guess how painful it is for you to see your sister like this."

"I'm so worried!"

The man stooped so that his face was on a level with hers. "Jessica, we're doing everything we can for Elizabeth. We're trying our best to make her well. Do you understand what I'm saying?"

She nodded mutely. Did he mean Elizabeth was going to be OK, or—something too horrible to imagine. . . .

"My name is John Edwards. I'm the neurosurgeon on your sister's case."

"Dr. Edwards?"

"That's right, Jessica. Your sister is in a coma. You know what that is, don't you?"

"It means Liz is going to die!" Jessica's voice cracked, and she couldn't hold back the tears any longer. She sobbed as if her heart were breaking.

She felt strong hands on her shoulders, shaking her gently but insistently. "Stop it, Jessica. Crying isn't going to help your sister. Elizabeth needs your strength, not your tears."

130

Jessica raised a tearstained face. "You don't understand!"

"I know how upset you are."

"You don't understand, Dr. Edwards," she said again. "It's my fault, all my fault!"

"Jessica, were you driving the car that hit the motorcycle?"

"No, of course not!"

"Then why is it your fault?" he asked kindly.

"Because I was supposed to give her a ride! I was selfish and left without her so she had to go with Todd on his motorcycle. If I'd waited, she wouldn't. . . . Oh, I should have waited. It *is* my fault!"

Suddenly Dr. Edwards's hands were cupping her face, forcing her to look up. "Jessica, accidents happen. They aren't anyone's fault. And right now, blame isn't important. Guiding Elizabeth back to all of you is! That's what we have to do. You and your brother and your parents have to bring Elizabeth back. I'll help, Jessica, but it's really up to you."

"Me?"

"Yes. You're the person closest to her. *You* have the best chance of reaching her. Talk to her. Just talk to her. Doctors can keep people alive with machines, but we can't will them to come back to us. Sometimes it doesn't matter how much you or I want it. The only thing we can do is try."

"I'll try. I'll do anything for Liz."

After the doctor had left, Jessica looked down at Elizabeth's quiet figure.

"Liz, can you hear me? Please, Lizzie. It was my fault you got hurt. Lizzie, I promise to

131

be more responsible in the future. But I can't do it without you. Liz, I need you so much!"

But the figure on the bed remained motionless.

Jessica rested her head on the bed, exhausted. She'd spent all day crying about Elizabeth. And every time someone tried to comfort her, she cried even more. This was the most horrible thing that had ever happened to her. She felt absolutely powerless; there was nothing she could to do help her sister, and the sight of Elizabeth, her life slowly draining away, was more than she could bear.

Jessica heard the door open behind her and looked up. Alice Wakefield had entered the room. Jessica jumped up and threw her arms around her mother. "Oh, Mom, I'm so scared!" she sobbed, tears streaming down her face again.

"Jess, honey, don't cry like this. Elizabeth isn't going to die. We won't let her! You'll see, darling. She'll come out of this; and everything will be the same as it was before the accident."

Jessica wanted to believe her mother's words. She wished that she could turn back the clock and make Elizabeth well once again. But in her heart she knew that nothing would ever be the same.

☐	25143	**POWER PLAY #4**	$2.50
☐	25043	**ALL NIGHT LONG #5**	$2.50
☐	25105	**DANGEROUS LOVE #6**	$2.50
☐	25106	**DEAR SISTER #7**	$2.50
☐	25092	**HEARTBREAKER #8**	$2.50
☐	25026	**RACING HEARTS #9**	$2.50
☐	25016	**WRONG KIND OF GIRL #10**	$2.50
☐	25046	**TOO GOOD TO BE TRUE #11**	$2.50
☐	25035	**WHEN LOVE DIES #12**	$2.50
☐	24524	**KIDNAPPED #13**	$2.25
☐	24531	**DECEPTIONS #14**	$2.50
☐	24582	**PROMISES #15**	$2.50
☐	24672	**RAGS TO RICHES #16**	$2.50
☐	24723	**LOVE LETTERS #17**	$2.50
☐	24825	**HEAD OVER HEELS #18**	$2.50
☐	24893	**SHOWDOWN #19**	$2.50
☐	24947	**CRASH LANDING! #20**	$2.50

Prices and availability subject to change without notice.

Buy them at your local bookstore or use this convenient coupon for ordering.

Bantam Books, Inc., Dept SVH, 414 East Golf Road, Des Plaines, Ill. 60016

Please send me the books I have checked above. I am enclosing $_____
(please add $1.50 to cover postage and handling). Send check or money order
—no cash or C.O.D.'s please.

Mr/Mrs/Miss _____

Address_____

City_____ State/Zip_____

SVH—5/86

Please allow four to six weeks for delivery. This offer expires 11/86.

SWEET DREAMS are fresh, fun and exciting,—alive with the flavor of the contemporary teen scene—the joy and doubt of *first love*. If you've missed any SWEET DREAMS titles, from #1 to #100, then you're missing out on *your* kind of stories, written about people like *you*!

☐	24945	QUESTIONS OF LOVE #86 Rosemary Vernon	$2.25
☐	24824	PROGRAMMED FOR LOVE #87 Marion Crane	$2.25
☐	24891	WRONG KIND OF BOY #88 Shannon Blair	$2.25
☐	24946	101 WAYS TO MEET MR. RIGHT #89 Janet Quin-Harkin	$2.25
☐	24992	TWO'S A CROWD #90 Diana Gregory	$2.25
☐	25070	THE LOVE HUNT #91 Yvonne Green	$2.25
☐	25131	KISS & TELL #92 Janet Quin-Harkin	$2.25
☐	25071	THE GREAT BOY CHASE #93 Janet Quin-Harkin	$2.25
☐	25132	SECOND CHANCES #94 Nany Levinso	$2.25
☐	25178	NO STRINGS ATTACHED #95 Eileen Hehl	$2.25
☐	25179	FIRST, LAST, AND ALWAYS #96 Barbara Conklin	$2.25
☐	25244	DANCING IN THE DARK #97 Carolyn Ross	$2.25
☐	25245	LOVE IS IN THE AIR #98 Diana Gregory	$2.25
☐	25297	ONE BOY TOO MANY #99 Marian Caudell	$2.25
☐	25298	FOLLOW THAT BOY #100 Debra Spector	$2.25
☐	25366	WRONG FOR EACH OTHER #101 Debra Spector	$2.25
☐	25367	HEARTS DON'T LIE #102 Terri Fields	$2.25
☐	25429	CROSS MY HEART #103 Diana Gregory	$2.25
☐	25428	PLAYING FOR KEEPS #104 Janice Stevens	$2.25
☐	25469	THE PERFECT BOY #105 Elizabeth Reynolds	$2.25
☐	25470	MISSION: LOVE #106 Kathryn Maris	$2.25
☐	25535	IF YOU LOVE ME #107 Barbara Steiner	$2.25
☐	25536	ONE OF THE BOYS #108 Jill Jarnow	$2.25

Prices and availability subject to change without notice.

BANTAM
SHOP·AT·HOME
C·A·T·A·L·O·G

Special Offer
Buy a Bantam Book
for only 50¢.

Now you can order the exciting books you've been wanting to read straight from Bantam's latest listing of hundreds of titles. *And* this special offer gives you the opportunity to purchase a Bantam book for only 50¢. Here's how:

By ordering any five books at the regular price per order, you can also choose any other single book listed (up to $4.95 value) for only 50¢. Some restrictions do apply, so for further details send for Bantam's listing of titles today.

Just send us your name and address and we'll send you Bantam Book's SHOP AT HOME CATALOG!